"*What the hell have I ever done to you?*"

"Just—just being Jerome's brother is enough."

"How can an apparently well-balanced woman get so prejudiced?"

"He told me things about you, like..." Dared she? "You were—" Once again something made her hesitate.

"I was—?" His eyebrows arched, his lips twisted. "Go on."

"You cared nothing for others, particularly women. You took life as it came, kind of shrugging it off. You were as hard as granite and used every experience—women, Jerome said he meant—to the full, then put it—them—behind you and moved on to the next, and the next...."

"Wow!" It was a long-drawn-out, sarcastic sound. "Have I, in your opinion, lived up to my callous reputation?"

LILIAN PEAKE lives near the sea in England. Her first job was working for a mystery writer, employment that she says gave her an excellent insight into how an author functions. She went on to become a journalist and reported on the fashion world for a trade magazine. Later she took on an advice column, the writing of which contributed to her understanding of people's lives. Now she draws on her experiences and perception, not to mention a fertile imagination, to craft her many fine romances. She and her husband have three children.

Books by Lilian Peake

HARLEQUIN PRESENTS

1124—TAKE THIS WOMAN
1157—THE BITTER TASTE OF LOVE
1268—DANCE TO MY TUNE
1316—CLIMB EVERY MOUNTAIN
1485—IRRESISTIBLE ENEMY
1532—UNDERCOVER AFFAIR

HARLEQUIN ROMANCE

2404—PROMISE AT MIDNIGHT
2603—NIGHT OF POSSESSION
2614—COME LOVE ME
2651—A WOMAN IN LOVE

LILIAN PEAKE

Gold Ring of Revenge

Harlequin Books

TORONTO • NEW YORK • LONDON
AMSTERDAM • PARIS • SYDNEY • HAMBURG
STOCKHOLM • ATHENS • TOKYO • MILAN
MADRID • WARSAW • BUDAPEST • AUCKLAND

Harlequin Presents first edition August 1993
ISBN 0-373-11580-6

Original hardcover edition published in 1992
by Mills & Boon Limited

GOLD RING OF REVENGE

CHAPTER ONE

PUTTING down her suitcases, Rhea massaged her aching arms. Then, shifting her bulging shoulder-pack into a more secure position, she retrieved the cases and continued walking.

Anger had kept her going through all the hours that she had been travelling, and it was that same anger that spurred her on now, overriding the tiredness that seemed to increase with every step. In her suitcases she carried all the worldly possessions that fate, in the form of the law, financial establishments and other people's trickery, had allowed her to keep.

Now she was on her way to find someone, a man who, she had been told on reliable authority, cared nothing for others, and women in particular; who was harder in nature than granite and who took life as it came, using it to the full and, when he had drained dry that particular experience—for 'experience', she had been advised, read 'woman'—putting it, and her, out of his mind and his life, moving on to the next . . . and the next.

She wished she knew where to look for him. He lived, she had been vaguely told, here in this village in the Yorkshire Dales. Its name was Cuttingbeck, but there was no one around from whom she could ask directions. Not a soul walked along the dusty road, nor stood in any doorway in the fitful sunshine.

As she walked, her feet dragging now with tiredness, a sound impinged on her ears. It rang like iron striking iron, hammering and pounding, then stopping with a clatter. Skylarks sang in brilliant chorus overhead and from behind a gate in a flower-filled cottage garden a dog barked fiercely.

The rhythmic hammering started again and, city-influenced though her hearing was, it could still interpret the meaning of those sounds. They told her that, somewhere nearby, there just had to be a forge, a blacksmith's, maybe, with someone working there from whom she could ask the way.

Optimism being an essential part of her character, she felt her heart lift at the prospect of an end to her journey—a long train-ride northwards from the environs of London. After which, having missed the bus with, apparently, a wait of three hours until the next one, she had had no real alternative but to start out on the three-mile walk which, she had been informed by a station attendant dubiously eyeing her baggage, stretched between that station and the village of Cuttingbeck.

Now and then she had rested, even climbing over a padlocked farm gate and falling asleep with utter weariness in the breezy sunshine in the corner of a field. After a series of sleepless nights, not to mention weeks of hassle and worry and emotional devastation, fatigue had finally caught up with her.

Unfortunately, as she had climbed back to the road, the old and rickety iron gate had rocked beneath her and her foot, having found a precarious perch on a bar, slipped and twisted awkwardly as it hit the ground. She had dropped to join it, rocking to and fro with the pain, then, biting her lower lip, rested back on a suitcase, hugging her throbbing foot.

Pausing now, putting her weight on her undamaged leg, Rhea tried to locate the place from which the hammering, which had stopped again, had come. To her relief it was resumed, and she traced it to the ancient stone-built barn which stood only a few yards distant. So the man—it had to be a man, because, she reasoned, surely no woman possessed such strength as the person working inside that building appeared to have—had not gone away.

Hovering in the open doorway, she saw the man pause as he leaned over the anvil, hammer held aloft, postponing the strike as if he had become conscious of the presence of another human being—had she perhaps cut off some of his light?—but unwilling to shift his eye from where it was pinpointed, and turn to investigate.

She hadn't said a word, had scarcely breathed, but the strike was abandoned and the hammer lowered. The man looked over his shoulder, registered her presence and turned fully to face her.

It was a moment which, to Rhea, seemed to be frozen in time. She would never forget her first sight of him. He was tall, with thick black hair, and stripped to the waist, his torso highlighted and outlined by the fire burning in the wide, blackened grate behind him. He was lean, yet muscled, his waistband sitting low over hips that boasted not even a pinch of spare flesh.

'Yes?' The hammer found a clattering place on a wooden table, the coke fire spitting as if irritated by the workman's straying attention.

Rhea tried to speak but found her lips were dry. Moving her tongue across them, she cleared her throat. 'I'm sorry to have interrupted you, but——'

He reached for a black T-shirt, pulling it on, then strolled towards her, hands in the pockets of his work-grimed trousers. It was then that she felt the full force of his eyes. They were a steely grey, piercing and telling of a formidable intellect, revealing an interest that was disinterested yet coldly sensual, but whose message held no gladness. Will you tell me what you want, it said, then go.

Near as she was now, Rhea became aware of how his neck and arms gleamed with a moisture imparted by the heat from the flicking flames, combined with the sheer physical effort the man had been expending. His upper lip held a sheen which clung to the dark roughness of a jaw that seemed not to have felt the scrape of a razor for a good many hours.

His eyes lowered to the suitcases she had dropped to the ground, taking in her shoulder-bag and her untidy brown hair, noting her general dishevelment. She held his gaze and, despite the extraordinary havoc it was causing inside her, tried to read his reaction, but found only an uninformative blankness.

'I'm sorry to interrupt you,' she said again, 'but I'm new to the area,' a self-evident statement which, she supposed, merited the faintly satirical flick of his brow, 'and I'm looking for someone. There was no one else around to ask, so I took a chance and came over here.' Do I have to babble so? she reproached herself, but the man's whole demeanour seemed to have reduced to rubble her powers of verbal self-censorship. 'His name is Leo Dower, and I'm told he lives in Cuttingbeck. I wondered if you'd heard of him?'

The faintest pause, then, 'I've heard.'

Despite her injured ankle, which had begun to ache alarmingly, a smile of sheer relief lit her face. 'So maybe you could direct me to his house?' He let the question hang in the air and she wondered if it was his way of saying no. 'I—I desperately need to talk to him——'

'Business or——' his eyes did a quick raking job and Rhea's reflexes quivered with a cocktail-mix of both excitement and anger '—pleasure?'

She could not stop the hectic flush. Male this man certainly was, but, instead of his innuendo annoying her as it should, to her consternation it made her heart beat faster.

'Certainly not the latter,' she returned indignantly, 'but,' her shoulders lifted, 'I suppose it could be categorised as business. His br——' Just in time, she stopped herself. She had no intention of giving away any more than necessary to this arrogant, not to say abrasive stranger.

His eyes flicked with a faint disparagement to her cases. 'You look as if you've come to stay for a year. Is this man expecting you?' His voice was even and cultured, bearing no overtones of a regional accent.

'Well, no, but... Anyway, I've got no intention of dumping myself on him uninvited. In all the circumstances, I'm sure he'd find me very unwelcome. I thought I might book a room at the local pub. Or find somewhere that does bed and breakfast.'

A piece of coke rearranged itself meaningfully, then hissed and flared. It seemed to be calling the man back to his work.

'OK.' He appeared to relent, approaching the doorway, brushing past Rhea, whose skin through her cotton jacket prickled alarmingly as his bare arm made fleeting contact with hers.

He lifted that arm and pointed. It was, Rhea noted in passing, liberally sprinkled with a layer of dark hair. 'See that rough track along the street, branching off to the left? It goes down to the river. Cross by the stone bridge—you see it?—and his cottage is just off to the left. You can't miss it.' He turned back to her. 'He won't be there, but don't let that worry you. Just open the door and walk in.' His smile mocked her worried frown. 'It's the custom in these parts.'

'He won't mind?'

'Believe me, he's not the kind of guy to worry one way or the other.' His gaze moved to her hair and, with a curiously familiar movement that unnerved her, his hand reached out, his fingers plucking at the deep brown strands and making a capture. He held it up. 'Grass? How come?'

There was no need for her to explain, but she did. 'When you feel you can't take another step without a rest,' she told him, reluctant to confide any weakness to a man with such obvious strength, both of body and mind, 'you find somewhere, anywhere, to do what your brain, and your body, tell you. I saw an empty field. My feet and legs took over from there.'

Plainly comprehending, he moved his mouth in the semblance of a smile. Thanking him for his directions, Rhea picked up her cases.

He was pulling off his T-shirt even before she moved away, seemingly anxious to return to his work. She felt that he watched her as she followed his directions, her tired legs dragging as she forced her painful foot to take its share of her weight, not to mention the burden of her cases, resisting the urge to turn round to check whether her suspicion was correct.

A silver birch, moving gracefully in full summer green, lifted itself high by the bank of the boulder-strewn river which passed within a forceful stone's throw of the cottage.

The road went on its winding way up the hill that led across the bare moorland, but, obeying instructions, Rhea descended from the bridge, leaving the road by an uneven track which led down to a lawn whose boundary was the stone-strewn path bordering the river.

Pausing, she looked at the cottage—more of a rambling two-storeyed house, really—with its slate-covered roof, its stone-silled windows tall and wide, a trellised archway interwoven with wild roses embellishing the main entrance door.

'Just open the door and walk in,' he'd said, so she did just that, but knocking first, in case the owner had returned without the stranger's knowledge.

Silence greeted Rhea's tentative, 'Mr Dower, are you home?' To make quite sure, she repeated the question, louder this time, but again there was no reply. The cases thumped from her stiffened fingers, her shoulder-pack hitting the carpet beside them, her undamaged leg again taking the strain.

The owner of the cottage, judging by its furnishings, well used but of good quality, was most decidedly not poverty-stricken, but this she already knew. Something inside her responded appreciatively to the countrified fabrics covering the sofa and easy-chairs, the theme followed through in the curtains, all but one of which remained pulled across from the night before.

With a sense of daring, Rhea limped round a low wooden table, a rack from which magazines spilled, and a couple of footstools piled high with books, and pushed wide the curtains covering the remaining window. The late afternoon sunlight flooded in, filling the room and dazzling her tired vision, making her acutely aware of her own fatigue.

Looking around, the feeling still strong of having trespassed, she sank on to a sofa, glad most of all to be able to rest her throbbing ankle. Only now did she allow herself to lift her trouser leg and inspect the damage, aghast at what she found. Her ankle had swollen, her foot, likewise, having become puffy and increasingly difficult to move within her shoe.

Rhea knew she should bathe it, bandage it even, but felt she had no right to do even that in a stranger's house. When she had found somewhere to stay, she told herself reassuringly, she would try and repair the damage with some plaster from the small first-aid kit she carried with her.

The tranquillity that came with the peace and quiet all around her was to her troubled senses like a stroking, soothing hand, although, closing her eyes, she could not prevent her thoughts from turning in on themselves.

The past returned like a slow-motion playback, but not in colour. It was all in black and white, with the brightness turned down and the contrast badly adjusted, the pictures that followed each other in relentless procession comfortless and bleak.

'What use are you to me now?' a man's voice said. 'Why should I hang around now there's nothing in it for me? What have you got to offer except what all women have got? And most of them know what to do with it a darn sight better than you.'

'But right from the start,' she whispered back, horrified and totally unbelieving, 'you said you loved me.'

'Of course I said that. What man wouldn't, to a girl with all that lovely money behind her? Devoted parents, her rich daddy doting on her, naming her his heiress. Some heiress!' He seized her shoulders, half shaking her. 'And to think I held off all that time, because "Mummy and Daddy" were so strait-laced and old-fashioned that they might ban me from their sight, not to mention their daughter's life. So I reminded myself every time I got within smooching distance and nearly overstepped the mark that Rhea Hirst's future fortune was worth holding off for.'

'Why, you——!' She tore away and lifted her hand, stinging his cheek. In his fury, his lips had almost disappeared, but she hid her fear and stood her ground. 'Get out,' she spat, 'out of this house and out of my life. I never want to see you again!'

'That's OK with me, pal,' he answered, and ran outside, getting into her car, firing the engine with the keys with which she had entrusted him. 'If you want this great bit of engineering back,' his hand came through the opened window and stroked the car's bodywork, 'contact me through my solicitor. Except that he won't tell.'

The engine roared under the pressure of his foot. 'If you want payment for this car,' he shouted, 'my brother will oblige. He's rolling in it.' He reached into a pocket and threw an envelope through the window. 'There's his address. But give him warning that you're coming, won't you? Otherwise you might walk into an embarrassing situation. He just *loves* the opposite sex. But I've told

you that before, haven't I? 'Bye, Rhea. Thanks for all
the happy memories we never had!'

Tearing off her engagement ring, she ran across and
hurled it into the car through the open window, then
watched helplessly as her own car—it had become hers
when her father had died, being all that she had managed
to salvage from the wreck of her life—became a mere
speck in the distance.

She awoke to sounds that seemed to be muted so as not
to awaken, a disturbance of air cooling her and making
her aware of the dampness on her cheeks. With the back
of her hand she tried to brush it away, but her eyes
seemed to be intent on supplying yet more.

A shuddering sob came from her depths as she awoke
fully and the figure of a man floated into her still misty
vision. He was staring down at her with neither con-
demnation nor welcome, nor even with surprise... Of
course he wasn't surprised to see her, she told herself
sharply. This was the man, wasn't it, who had directed
her to this cottage? But, judging by the taut line of his
mouth, he seemed more foe than friend. Swinging her
legs to the floor, she sat upright.

'Are you Leo Dower?' she demanded.

'I'm Leo Dower.'

'Why,' she challenged, 'when I spoke to you in the
forge, didn't you tell me who you were? Why did you
pretend to be someone else?'

His smile held no mirth. 'I didn't want you to turn
and run. There are too many questions needing answers,
Miss Hirst. Like, where's my brother Jerome?'

'You know who I am?' Unsteadily she got to her feet,
surreptitiously favouring her uninjured foot. His hand
reached out, the back of it succeeding in reducing the
dampness on her cheeks where hers had failed.

'Nursing a secret sorrow?' he queried, with more
cynicism than sympathy.

She shrank from the contact, slight though it had been, but the smooth skin of her cheeks seemed to have a mind of its own. It retained the faint impact of his touch as if it had actually liked it.

'I know. Jerome sent me an assortment of photos, of you, of himself with his arm round you. An engagement portrait such as loving, if a mite old-fashioned parents demand.'

His hair was damp, which indicated that he had showered while she had slept. He pushed his hands into the waistband of the dark trousers into which he had changed. His potent cleanliness made her even more conscious of her dust-laden self, and she found herself longing for a bath, for a change of clothes, for a mirror. Then she'd be able to tidy her long hair and apply a little make-up and show this sardonic individual that she had more feminine attractions than at that moment he seemed to consider she possessed.

'So where's Jerome?' he pursued.

'I wish I knew, Mr Dower,' she snapped. 'He owes me—oh, yes, he owes me. If I ever come across him again, I'll make him pay—oh!'

A cry escaped her and she fell forward, her face crumpling with pain. He caught her, holding her away from him by her arms. Rhea cursed herself for her stupidity. Forgetfully she had put some weight on to her injured foot, and the agony was such that she felt she could hardly bear it.

All the same, with her head rigidly high, she braced her shoulders to pull from his hold, refusing to display any kind of weakness in front of this macho, sardonic creature. But through sheer force of habit she used the damaged foot yet again and, with an anguished gasp, fell against him. This time he permitted the contact, tolerating her arms as they clamped for support around his waist.

Her head drooped this time, her cheek of its own accord finding a resting place against his chest, the drumming of his heart beneath her ear reminding her of the rhythmic hammering she had heard as she had approached the forge.

An image of his torso, moist and tough and muscled as it had been when she had first set eyes on him, flashed before her eyes, and a strange excitement coursed through her, a feeling she suppressed as fast as it had arisen.

'OK,' he eased her from him, 'you can switch off the righteous indignation. It takes two to land you in the mess you're in. So he's made you pregnant. When's the child due?'

She jerked away and stared up at him. 'What child?'

'Oh, come on, now, Miss Hirst, there's no need to be coy with me. I know my brother as if he were part of me.' He released her and she forced herself to remember to stand on her good leg. 'You think you're the first young woman in that kind of trouble that he's pointed in my direction?'

Rhea could only stare at him.

'So you're shocked, horrified at what I'm telling you,' he went on, plainly having no intention of sparing her. 'He'd given you a ring, you're thinking, which surely meant he was genuinely in love with you? He put on such an act of devotion you don't believe me?' He shook his head slowly. 'I know his ways. He's a smooth talker, my brother, the kind that women fall for by the dozen.'

'I think,' she answered fiercely, knowing she also had once fallen for that 'smooth talk', 'that you're the most arrogant, unpleasant-minded individual I've ever——'

'Let's be realistic, Miss Hirst.' There was a faint impatience in his tone. 'You think you're the first—er—lady to come running to me for that reason? Then think again.' He held up his hand, his fingers indicating four. 'So far, that is. You want payment for services ren-

dered? OK, as Jerome knows only too well, I'll oblige.
All the others went away satisfied with the sum of money
I offered them.'

'Oh! You're no different from your brother!' Her hand
itched to make stinging contact with his cheek as it had
with Jerome's. 'You're both as callous, as unscrupulous, as uncaring of people's feelings as each
other!'

'Uncaring?' He seemed really angry now. Those grey
eyes held the flash of steel. 'You call my offer of help
an *uncaring* act?'

Rhea took a sharp breath. Maybe he was right, maybe
in his own eyes he *was* doing his best to right the wrong
he thought his brother had inflicted.

If only she hadn't injured herself, she fretted. If only
she could pick up her belongings and walk out.

'You have the effrontery to call me callous,' he was
saying, 'when I'm doing the honest thing, uninvolved
though I am, and offering you cash as some kind of
reparation for the coming total disruption of your life—
brought about not by me, but by my brother?'

'Thank you for your kind gesture,' she answered
levelly, 'but——' There is no child, she had been about
to say, but at that moment her uninjured leg started
shaking under the stress of keeping her upright and she
sank back on to the sofa, white-faced with pain.

He frowned down at her, and she remembered that
he could not know the reason for her distress since the
leg of her jeans hid the swollen flesh around her foot
and ankle. If she could manage to stave off his intruding
questions and remain there for an hour or two until the
swelling subsided, she would probably be able to make
it to the local inn and in a few days make her
way...where?

In the depths of the nightmares that had followed
Jerome's departure, when she had felt so utterly alone,
the idea had taken root of seeking out this unknown

relative, as Jerome had suggested. Somebody in the Dower family owed her, and who better to make that payment than the brother called Leo?

'OK.' Leo's voice was hard. He plainly thought that her show of pain was staged for his benefit. 'Let's quit the melodramatic routine, shall we? Then you can tell me what it is you want.'

She knew now, beyond doubt, what she wanted. It was revenge—revenge for all the unhappiness and misery that his brother had inflicted on her... for the lies, the double dealing, the fraud he had perpetrated and the destitution she now found herself in, but, most of all, for the way he had emptied her life of feeling, of meaning, of love itself...

'Strange that my brother cast *you* adrift,' Leo was saying, arms folded, expression malely appreciative, although overlaid with a measure of contempt. 'Yet not strange. Amber eyes that should melt a man, yet they're cool enough to make him shiver. I wonder why.'

He considered her for a few moments.

'A face the shape of a heart,' he went on, 'but without the warmth that keeps that vital organ beating.' He shook his head. 'How can I believe what I've heard? That this time my little brother had hit the jackpot? He'd got himself engaged, he said, to a girl who had everything. Not only was she sexy, he told me, but she also had a fortune behind her. Provided, of course, he said, that he was nice to her daddy and watched his step by playing the old-fashioned gentleman, in public at least, towards the daughter whom the father, not to mention the mother, worshipped.'

Hearing Jerome's exact sentiments confirmed by this pitiless man, hearing the truth as Jerome had so cruelly spelled it out in the weeks following her parents' deaths, hit Rhea like a hammer blow. She would, she vowed, get even with the Dower family as unscrupulously, as calculatedly, as its younger son had robbed her, Rhea Hirst, of all that she had held most dear.

'Except,' Leo Dower went on, his dark gaze raking her, 'it's plain he didn't keep to his resolve. I could never in a million years imagine my brother playing the "gentleman" where his girlfriends...I beg your pardon,' with sardonic courtesy, 'fiancées...are concerned.'

The telephone rang distantly and Leo, with a brief 'Excuse me', opened a door which, Rhea noted with a turn of the head, appeared to lead into an inner hall. Stairs could be glimpsed rising to the upper floor. Her heart sank. In pain as she was, how could she hope to make it up that staircase to the bathroom?

'Sonya!' His voice carried clearly, and to Rhea's ears there was no mistaking the softening of his tone. 'The gates are coming along fine. Timmy thinks he's cracked the problem of the mechanism. Tonight? Well, maybe, maybe not. I'll get back to you on that.'

There was a pause and Rhea could see Leo's fine-shaped head turn in her direction as he leant against the wrought-iron rails of the banisters.

'I've got a "problem" of my own right now,' he went on. Rhea was sure she heard a high-pitched groan. 'Yeah, another of Jerome's cast-offs has just presented herself on my doorstep.' He had made no attempt to lower his voice. 'Strangle my brother?' He laughed, and it was such a good sound that it sent shivers up and down Rhea's spine. 'Maybe I will one day. As you and I know, he does have this compulsion to keep proving his virility... One more of his little bundles of joy sent my way and I might just, next time, send the lady back and force Jerome to face up to his responsibilities and the consequences of his actions.' He turned away, lowering his voice at last and conversing about private matters.

How I wish, Rhea fretted, wincing at the pain in her foot which, instead of receding, was growing by the minute, I could go right over to that door and slam it shut. So the macho older version of Jerome Dower was still convinced she was in 'that certain condition'? Let him, she thought, her head resting back, her mind trying to fight the agony her injury was causing, not only to her foot now, but to the rest of her body.

It didn't matter what he thought, because before long she would be on her way again, although heaven knew where. It was obvious that her journey had been in vain. Leo Dower knew no more of Jerome's whereabouts than she did. Which meant that he couldn't retrieve her car from his brother's illegal possession any more than she could. But, she admitted again, all these things had not been the only reason why she had made the trek northward to a man she had never met.

A curious kind of instinct, dredged up from beneath the floor of her subconscious mind, coupled with an overpowering intuition, had instilled in her a conviction that, after the upheaval and the turmoil that life in the past few months had flung at her, the place she was travelling towards, unknown to her though it might be, was a kind of blissful sanctuary, beckoning her on.

CHAPTER TWO

'IF YOU'D like to freshen up,' Leo Dower stood before her, hands in the pockets of his dark trousers, 'the bathroom's up the stairs. Unless you've already found your way there?'

Rhea shook her head. 'Do you,' she asked, her fingers crossed, 'have a cloakroom downstairs?'

He looked faintly puzzled, then shrugged. 'If you'll follow me, I'll show you.'

Gritting her teeth, Rhea made to stand, tentatively putting some weight on her injured ankle. She just managed to suppress a shriek, but a strangled gasp of pain did escape her throat. She knew then that she couldn't make it anywhere, not a single step, under her own steam. What was more, she had to face the appalling fact that it would take more than the couple of hours she had estimated for the swelling, which was now crowding her shoe to bursting point, to go down.

'What the hell——?' He had returned to stand in front of her as she sank on to the sofa again. She unintentionally glanced down, and he followed her gaze. Crouching, he lifted her left foot, the undamaged one, then pushed up the other trouser-leg.

'Please,' she gasped, white-faced, 'just—just don't touch it!'

'For...God's...sake!' He stared at the ankle and Rhea saw with horror the size it had swelled to. 'How far did you count on going with that?' His hands sprang to action, sliding beneath her, easing her body sideways so that her legs were resting on the sofa.

His tone might have been harsh, Rhea reflected abstractedly, but his hands which, as she had witnessed from the door of the forge, possessed the strength to hammer and bend and fashion objects out of iron, were so gentle that she almost wept.

A couple of tears did escape, she could not stop them. She had been tired before, but fatigue plus agony was, as she was discovering, almost too much to bear.

Leo stood abruptly, fingers spread on hips, jaw thrust forward, eyes narrowed. 'When?' he asked. 'Where and how?'

Haltingly, she explained how she had rested in the corner of a field. 'As I climbed back, the gate wobbled under me. It was loose on its hinges and rusty, and my foot lost its hold when the bar I was standing on broke. The gate went over with me. I did rest it back into place in case the sheep got out, but——'

'You mean you carried on walking?'

'I had no alternative, had I? Anyway, it didn't hurt quite so much then.' She turned away. 'I'm sorry—it's not really your concern. Just drive me to the nearest pub or hotel and I'll take it from there.'

'The nearest hospital, more like it,' he countered grimly. His hands slid under her again and he lifted her, making for the inner hall.

'Where——?' she asked, holding her head stiffly upright, then realised with some embarrassment just where he was taking her. He pushed at the cloakroom door with his foot and slid her down. She stood on her uninjured leg, her hand against the wall.

'Call when you're ready,' he threw over his shoulder as he walked away.

Beneath her pallor, her skin was suffused with pink. Tough and hard his exterior might seem, she thought, not to mention the inner man too, but he didn't seem quite as devoid of finer feelings as Jerome had made him out to be.

'Where are you taking me?' she asked a few moments later as he put her into his car, a low-slung, clearly expensive vehicle which stood in the rear yard that gave on to the road.

'The nearest hospital. I rang the local doctor and I'm taking his advice.'

'But, Mr Dower,' she protested, 'there's no need for you to put yourself out like this. I wished myself on you. I'm not even an invited guest.'

'What kind of a guy do you think I am that you assume I can ditch you, my brother's girlfriend, in the condition you're in?'

What condition? she wanted to ask, but decided to let it go. The answer was obvious anyway. Closing her eyes, she felt the pain wash over her.

The second time Rhea walked into Leo Dower's house, she was on crutches. 'There's no need for you to stay,' she had told him as they had waited for attention at the hospital.

He hadn't even deigned to answer, striding about the waiting area, picking up, skimming through and discarding magazines, and staring through the windows as ambulances came and went.

Once or twice he had come to sit beside her, throwing himself into the chair as if it had done him an injury. Rhea had felt she couldn't blame him for resenting the situation into which she had plunged him, but if it hadn't been for his brother, she had reasoned, she wouldn't be there at all, would she?

Now he walked beside her, watching her slow, uncomfortable progress as she gritted her teeth and did her very best to keep her foot, which a cast now embraced from knee almost to toes, from any contact with the ground. It was no easy matter, she discovered, doing even such a simple thing as lowering herself into a chair.

Hands in pockets, Leo looked down at her, and as she raised her head and sought his eyes she felt again the same kind of shock as she had experienced at their first encounter. Try as she might, however, she still could not read his thoughts. But, she told herself, she didn't need to, did she?

Being apparently too polite to express his feelings in words, inwardly he was almost certainly cursing her presence, not to mention her link with his brother. No doubt he was trying to work out a way of ridding himself of her as quickly as he could arrange it.

'Thank you for all you've done,' she said, to put his mind at rest about her immediate intentions. 'Now, if you would be kind enough to give me a drink of water, then take me to the hotel——'

'What hotel?'

'As you can see, I'm able to walk now,' she gestured to the crutches, 'after a fashion. I don't expect it will take me long to learn to manoeuvre myself up and down the stairs. So——'

He stood unmoving, just staring down.

'I can't stay here,' she remonstrated, her voice rising, 'not for the two weeks they said I'd have to keep the plaster on.'

'Do you really believe I'd turn my brother's fiancée out?'

'I'm *not* his fiancée,' she cried, 'nor even his girl-friend. Don't you understand? He's stolen my car, taken things that I really value that I'd packed in it. Not only that, I'll never forgive him for all the other things he's done. He's wrecked my life, he's——'

'OK, OK, he's a miserable swine. That's what the others called him. I've heard it all before.' Leo's broad shoulders lifted and fell. 'If you'll excuse my saying so,' he said coldly, 'if women—and, apparently, you are no exception—are so stupid as to line up to be ill-used and pushed around by types like my brother—who, to me, is so transparently out only for his own ends—that's their fault. What puts my back up is that he always sends them to me to pick up the pieces.'

'You,' Rhea raged, goaded almost beyond endurance by his dismissive manner, 'are just as unfeeling and uncaring as your brother, except that you're even more macho. I *hate* him, do you understand? And because you're so like him in character, I——'

'You hate me too.' Another shrug. 'I can take it. Why don't you recite the usual list of accusations? I'm a cold fish, heartless, made of stone, et cetera. Take it or leave it, that's my way. All the same, you're staying here.' He went through into the inner hall, returning with the water she had asked for.

She drank thankfully and greedily. It was the first liquid that had passed her lips since very early that morning.

'Another?' He took the proffered glass, smiling faintly as she nodded. 'It seems I might have to warn the water authorities to be on the alert in case the reservoirs run dry.' He returned with the filled glass. 'There's a bed made up in the guest room. You can have that. And,' his hand thrust out, covering her mouth as she made to protest, 'you should have told my brother "no", shouldn't you, before he landed you in your present mess?'

Once again she frowned, about to ask, What mess? when once again she realised what he was implying. She stayed silent. Even if she told him, she reasoned, that there was no way he could be right in his assumption about her 'condition', that there had been no true intimacy between her and Jerome because Jerome had had his own selfish, and self-interested reasons, Leo Dower wouldn't have believed her.

Their evening meal over, Leo stood, hands in his pockets, and looked down at her. He had cooked the food, carrying in a low table so that Rhea could eat from it while still seated on the sofa. He had joined her and, having switched on the television, consumed his meal while watching a programme about the history of art.

'I won't apologise for the informality,' he had said, looking a little mockingly at her from across the room, 'but it's my way. Belonging to the moneyed classes as you do——'.

Rhea shook her head. 'Did. Past tense.'

His cynical smile dismissed her statement. 'If my easygoing ways go against the grain—your grain, then——' An expressive shrug dismissed any objections she hadn't even thought of making.

Now she said, 'There's no need to look at me as if you'd like to send me down the nearest rubbish chute. If you want to keep your date with your lady friend, please don't let me stop you.'

His eyebrows flicked up and down, then he seemed to make up his mind. Surprising her, he bent to pick up the container of painkillers which the hospital had prescribed, shook out two on to a paper tissue he had pulled from a nearby box and left them on the low table. 'For you, should you need them in my absence,' he said. Then he pocketed the container.

'You can stop looking outraged,' he added, rattling the confiscated tablets. 'It's merely a precautionary measure.'

'But I'm not like that,' she protested. 'In my view, life is for the living. And I'm a fighter. I don't give in to adverse circumstances——'

'I had noticed,' he commented drily.

'And,' she went on, 'no matter how much of a mess my life might be in I'd never take anything that might bring it to a premature end. I assure you, Mr Dower——'

'For God's sake,' he broke in irritably, 'make it Leo. I am, after all, almost your brother-in-law.' She started to protest that he was so wrong, for some strange reason not liking the 'brother' idea one little bit, but he went on unperturbed,

'Maybe you wouldn't take drastic measures—in your normal state, but bearing the scars as you do of my brother's misuse, I'm taking no chances. The others who came here——'

'But I'm not——'

'Not like them? I'm taking no chances.'

I'm not pregnant, she had been going to confess at last, but he had prevented her from doing so. It was her business anyway, she told herself. 'If it makes you happy,' she tossed at him with a long-suffering sigh, leaning back.

He considered her again, and under his intense scrutiny she felt her toes curling and her palms growing moist. There was an electric quality in his eyes, something in them that made her squirm and twist inside, then let the tension snap, reaching out and . . .

'Before you go,' she burst out, wanting to distract his attention from her and to give herself time to bring her wayward reactions back under her reason's calmer control, 'would you mind bringing me a glass of water, in case I need to take the two tablets you've been so *kind* as to allow me to keep?'

He obliged, from the door advising her with a half-smile not to get drunk on it.

Rhea's head sank back and she let the silence of the empty cottage wash over her. Her reaction to Leo Dower both puzzled and worried her, and she wished more than ever that she had been able to walk out of his life as easily as she had walked into it.

Staying right where she was, she knew instinctively, held greater dangers than the world outside could ever offer. Danger to her equilibrium, which she had only just regained after her devastating experiences at the hands of authority and the powers-that-be, and, most of all, one man's unscrupulous behaviour.

Also, danger to her future well-being, not physical, but to her inner peace, which she was still struggling to rediscover, but which so far had eluded her. One thing she knew for certain: the man who had just walked out of the door wouldn't give that peace back to her.

Operating the remote control, she tried to forget her troubles by concentrating on the film. In spite of everything, she found it so gripping that, when it was over, she returned with a shock to reality and pain. The grandfather clock told her from the inner hall that it was eleven o'clock. It also told her that the effect of the two painkilling tablets she had taken some hours before had worn off.

Swallowing the two that Leo had left her, she drank the water, then looked around. No man, she thought with unusual cynicism, would leave the arms of his lady love—and she was convinced that the lady called Sonya to whom he had gone was just that—before the early hours, if indeed the man in question ever left his lady before morning dawned.

Since she was too uncomfortable to stay where she was for the night, she gave the low table a small push to clear a space, then slowly swung first one leg, then the other, to the floor. Having encountered only a little pain, and therefore feeling pleased with herself, she reached for the crutches and levered herself to her feet.

She made straight for the stairs and, gritting her teeth, climbed painfully up them. Now and then she stopped for breath, forcing herself to look neither up, for discouragement, nor down, through fear, making it to the top, feeling beads of moisture on her forehead and clamminess in her hands.

Walking along the landing, by elimination she found the guest room. It was soberly furnished in browns and dark greens, its drapery practical rather than pretty. The bed, as Leo had claimed, had been made up, and she wondered how many overnight visitors he entertained that he found it worth his while to keep the room in a state of readiness.

In the bathroom along the landing she looked with longing at the tub, but in her present state there was no question even of using the shower. Washing herself as thoroughly as she could, she took a towel from a pile which she found on a chair.

By the time she had managed to remove her clothes, rummage about in her cases for a nightdress to wear, pulling it on and shifting herself sideways beneath the bedcover, she had, she discovered, used up every scrap of energy she hadn't even realised she possessed.

Bed was a haven, a paradise of softness, and she sank back, totally exhausted, into its welcoming comfort. But, try as she might, sleep escaped capture. The events of the day built up in her mind, brick on relentless brick, into a wall that had to be scaled before the longed-for state of unconsciousness was achieved that would give her respite from the pain of her injury and rest from the commotion of her thoughts.

There was the rustle of the breeze through leaves and the sound of water flowing, which told Rhea that the guest room overlooked the river, and was therefore at the rear of the cottage. There were other night sounds too, unfamiliar to her suburban-accustomed ear, sounds which were no doubt natural to the countryside, but which caused a *frisson* of fear to run down her spine.

The scrunch of car wheels swerving to a halt on the parking area at the front of the house made her still-alert brain go into overdrive. Despite the fact that her reason told her that, since midnight had just struck on the clock downstairs, it was probably Leo returning, her imagination, in conspiracy with her almost helpless state, made her fingers grasp the bedcover in a trembling hold.

As swift footsteps took the stairs, she forced herself to face the truth—that it hadn't really been the fear of an unknown stranger intruding with ill intent, but the imminent reappearance on her particular scene of her host, Leo Dower. In her tired and defenceless state, she felt unequal to him in every way.

'Miss Hirst,' he shouted, 'where the hell——? Rhea——?'

All she could do was to stare as Leo Dower strode into the room. 'It's you,' she managed hoarsely, her mouth dry with the fear that hadn't completely left her.

'Of course it's me,' he threw back, hands on hips. 'Who else could it be? Or did you hope it was Jerome returned to hug you to his penitent bosom?'

Rhea stared back at him, resenting his vigour, which had not diminished in spite of the late hour, the muscularity of his build which, because of his height, he carried so easily, the powerful life flowing through him which, unless she built impregnable sea defences around the turbulent femininity within her, might break out and surge towards her, swamping her totally.

'Tell me something,' he said conversationally, folding his arms, but Rhea was sure that underneath his smooth manner there was more than a spark of irritation, 'how did you get yourself into this bed?'

'Well,' she returned, aware that she was being provocative, 'no knight on a white charger came to my rescue and carried me here. I proceeded upward in the usual way. I trod one stair at a time——'

'Don't try and be clever, Rhea. Suppose you'd missed your step, or fallen?'

'Don't worry; because I as good as wished myself on you, I wouldn't have sued,' she retorted, wishing he would go. With her barriers down and fatigue clamouring to be indulged, as each second passed he seemed to her to take on the substance of a great rock to which she might cling in the aftermath of the storms which had so recently battered to pieces her life as she had known it.

His lips thinned at her provocative reply, but he stayed silent. Then it occurred to her just why he was so concerned about her well-being. She gave a mental shrug. If he chose to classify her with those others he kept referring to—his brother's 'cast-offs', he had scathingly called them—then that was his prerogative.

Anyway, she decided, now was not the time to let the truth come pouring out. The story was a long one, with many twists and turns, and, anyway, it seemed that he couldn't bear to hear one word spoken against his beloved brother. And she had, she reflected, so much to hold against Jerome Dower that it would fill a book.

It was late too, and she could hardly keep her eyes open. The painkilling tablets seemed finally to be taking effect and sleep beckoned at last.

'If you really want to know,' she murmured drowsily, shutting him out, 'it was sheer will-power that got me up here. I told you,' her eyes fluttered open, but she could not see his expression because he had switched off the light, 'I'm a fighter. If I weren't, Mr Dower,' her voice was a tired whisper, 'I can assure you, I wouldn't be here now. I mean, in your house, with all I've got left in the world scattered around your guest room...'

Rhea knew he was puzzled by the tone of her voice. 'What happened to the alleged fortune?'

'"Alleged" is right, Mr Dower...'

Through the mists of the sleep that was claiming her, she heard him go.

She heard herself crying out, felt a hard hand shaking her, not roughly, but sufficiently to bring her out of the nightmare.

Her head was throbbing along with her heart and her injury. She was enfolded in arms that were tenderly strong, offering a haven from the terrible dream she had fought to get out of. She found herself succumbing to the seductive comfort of those arms, letting them take over her problems, solving them and offering the security and love she had so recently lost.

In unbuttoned shirt and trousers which he seemed to have hastily pulled on, Leo sat sideways on the bed. His face was so near that, despite the half-light, Rhea could see the ruggedness of his eyebrows, the way his nostrils flared, the thick sensuality of his lips... And as if that weren't enough, there was the fine mat of chest hair, the muscular fitness of his torso...

'What are you doing?' he growled. 'Fantasising that I'm Jerome and willing me to kiss you as he must have done many times? So why not oblige a lady by acting out her fantasy, hm?'

His broad shoulders had shrugged as he had spoken, and Rhea could detect in their action the character of the man as his brother had described it. Harder than granite, Jerome had said, taking women and leaving them, taking life as it came, with not an atom of sentiment inside him.

All this time he had been lowering his mouth towards hers. Her head had had plenty of time to turn itself away, her mouth to take avoiding action, her body to stiffen, but none of those things happened. Instead, her hypnotised eyes watched his lips approach, her brain recognising the consequences, but giving out no frantic signals to avoid them at all costs.

He had slipped his arms under her shoulders and they half lifted her the rest of the way, his lips touching lightly all over hers, then, without warning, pressing down and taking them over, prising open an entry and making free with all the welcome they found there and which for the life of her she had not been able to withhold.

Panic made her heartbeats thunder in her chest. This man, she told herself, shouldn't be doing this, he had no right—and, for the sake of her self-respect, she had no right to let him.

'What a foolish little brother I've got,' he commented, his voice dry, as he held her away and looked her over quizzically, 'to walk out on everything that *you* would be able to offer a man.'

So it had been a game to him, the kiss that had transported her to something very like the foothills of heavenly heights? It started then to register on Rhea's dazed brain that the owner of the arms that held her, that mouth which had relentlessly demolished her barriers and brought her dulled and deadened senses back to leaping life, was Jerome's brother, and as such as much her enemy as Jerome had become.

She began to struggle, attempting to extricate herself from his hold.

'Let me go,' she got out, panting with a residual excitement so pleasurable that it frightened her. 'I don't want any other member of the Dower family to touch me ever again!'

Another shrug—the action was becoming familiar—and Leo complied at once, letting her sink back on to the pillows. He pocketed his hands and stood tall and aloof and indifferent in the semi-darkness. She told herself agitatedly that, as he had disengaged from her, her body had *not* felt deprived and disappointed.

'You were screaming with fear,' he said tonelessly. 'You were crying out for your parents. You loved them, you said, and why did it have to happen?' His voice was so unemotional that it helped to banish the tears that would otherwise have started all over again. 'Where are they now?'

'My parents? They died,' she answered dully, 'in a plane crash.' She took a dragging breath. 'Their own plane—a small one. My father was at the controls. They were on their way to the South of France for a holiday, just the two of them. They never got there.'

He stayed silent, looking down at her, expression inscrutable.

'It's a recurring nightmare that I have,' she went on slowly. 'I dream I'm with them...' She turned her head away.

After a long silence, Leo said, 'And Jerome—afterwards, he left you? Despite the fact that you were bereaved, that you were carrying his——'

'He left me,' she broke in quickly, wishing he wouldn't keep referring to something that just was not true. 'He left me,' she repeated, 'taking my car and all the things I had packed in it. Which is why I came to you—to find him and get my property back. But it seems I was wasting my time, because you don't know his whereabouts either. So,' she sighed, longing to sleep now, 'as soon as I'm able to leave your house, I'll be on my way.'

'To—where?'

'Who knows? If I knew, Mr Dower, I'd tell you.'

Between his teeth he said, 'Leo.' There was a rattle of pills and he took her hand, apparently with the intention of placing two tablets on her palm. The sight of the diamonds sparkling in the half-light stopped him. 'Jerome's ring?' he asked sharply.

'No. I threw that back at him—literally.' His expression seemed to change and she guessed he was smiling. 'This belonged to my mother. She had a lot of jewellery—my father showered her with it. They were so in love.' Her voice wavered and she cleared her throat. 'Most of it went to pay off debts, but I managed to salvage some pieces. Some of it,' her voice cracked, 'was in the car that Jerome took.'

Leo swore under his breath. All this time he had not relinquished his hold on her hand. In spite of herself, and her statement that she wanted no more contact with anyone named Dower, Rhea found the gesture, impersonal though it was, strangely comforting. In all the unhappy weeks that had followed the loss of her parents, there had been no one to offer her sympathy and understanding. Advice and guidance and professional assistance in abundance, but no human warmth, nor comfort.

'Is the pain bad?' He indicated her injury.

'Yes,' she whispered. 'The bedcover—it seems so heavy.'

Two tablets dropped on to her palm and he went away, as she had guessed, to fetch water. 'Need help with taking them?'

He did not wait for her answer. Sliding his arm beneath her back, he eased her into a semi-sitting position. One by one she took the tablets and, thanking him, handed back the glass. He lowered her slowly, but something perverse inside her had not wanted the contact to end.

He went away again, returning with a pile of pillows. Pushing aside the bedcover, he placed them each side of her leg, draping the cover over them, easing down her nightdress which, to her embarrassment, had ridden high over her thighs. His quick glance at her flushed face told her nothing.

'That should help to take the weight,' he said. From the door, he added, 'You can stay here for as long as you like. The Dower family you so dislike owes you at least a roof over your head.'

'Please don't let *your* conscience be troubled by my circumstances, Mr——' he made a belligerent movement '—Leo,' she corrected. 'There's no need to take the sins of your sibling on to *your* shoulders.' Powerful and near-irresistible though they are, a wilful voice whispered. Resting your head on those could become habit-forming... He's worth two of Jerome, it persisted tormentingly.

'OK, Rhea,' he strolled indolently back, 'so you don't like the brothers Dower. You bear a grudge and you've declared war.' His glance slanted down to where her middle would be underneath the cover. 'I guess I can't blame you. But cut the sarcasm, will you? Because I could pay you back in the same coin, and lady, if I did, I'd carve you up inside.'

He had changed in a fraction of a second from friendly acquaintance to implacable enemy. Rhea had begun to look to him for a measure of reassurance, for some kind of security, for a helping hand in the wilderness.

Now she realised what a mistake she had made in letting his kindly actions encourage her to allow her feelings to come back to cautious life. She had sworn to hate him because of his relationship to Jerome. And hate him she would go on doing, because otherwise, her insight told her, she could well be hurt, torn apart, all over again.

She gritted her teeth in an effort to harden herself, then with dismay felt tears gather behind her eyes. Try though she did, by closing her eyelids tightly, nothing was able to stop the tears from spilling over.

There was a sound like breath catching, then he was bending over her. 'Look at me, Rhea.' He flicked the tears away with a hard-skinned finger. 'It's been a hell of a day for you, so we'll call a truce, hm?' His finger hooked under her chin and his mouth found hers again. But this time the kiss was like one passing between a concerned parent and a fretful child.

'I'm in the next room if you need me. Goodnight.'

CHAPTER THREE

RHEA woke late, so late that it was almost lunchtime. She lay there for a few moments listening to the country sounds—birdsong, the river's singing coming faintly in through the opened windows, a distant sheep bleating.

Together they combined to tranquillise and soothe, allowing her to forget for a few precious minutes the twin pains of past and present. Then, knowing she could not delay getting up any longer, she moved into action, taking her time, going out to the bathroom, reckoning on Leo's being out at work.

Which, as she discovered on descending the stairs, hanging on for dear life to the banisters with one hand while the other managed to hold the crutches, was right.

A note was propped against the toaster.

> Make free with whatever. For Pete's sake, don't starve yourself or the generation to come.

Her instinct was to crumple the paper because of its false assumption about her condition, but she spared it, reluctantly recognising its caring tone, even if it was tinged with the sarcasm he had promised to use against her should she try to use it first on him.

She was resting on the crutches in the centre of the living-room, wondering what to do with the rest of the day and hating the injury and pain that made her so immobile, when approaching footsteps made her stiffen. Leo had left his work to see how she was managing? More likely, she told herself acidly, to make sure she was not damaging any of his precious property.

36

'Hi.' A man of around forty stood in the doorway. Of medium height, sandy-haired, he was casually dressed, with a manner to match. He seemed surprised—no, Rhea thought, that was too mild a word. Astonished was more accurate. 'Oh, dear,' he seemed amused, 'what will Sonya say? I'm Nathan Oxley, Leo's friend.'

Rhea nodded, summoning a smile. 'Good morning, Mr Oxley—I'm Rhea Hirst. And the lady called Sonya need not "say" anything. I've no intention of supplanting her, or any other woman, in Leo Dower's affections.'

She hopped painfully towards the settee and with the help of the newcomer, who stepped swiftly across to offer a hand, sank down with some relief.

'You might as well know, since you say you're Leo Dower's friend,' she smiled tiredly up at him, 'that the family Dower tops my hate list.'

'Hey,' Nathan Oxley took her up, seating himself sideways on an upright chair, 'Leo's a great guy. What's he done to deserve such censure from a lady I've never heard him even mention before?'

'It isn't what *he* has done.' Rhea stroked the leg cast for something to do. 'It's what his brother's done...' Too late she realised the interpretation he would put on such a statement, and, from his slightly embarrassed expression, she knew he had.

For heaven's sake, she thought, how many other girls had Jerome sent packing as he'd finally sent her? And *she* had been engaged to him...

'Jerome. Ah.' Nathan's pause spoke volumes. 'But surely,' he frowned at the cast, 'Jerome wasn't also responsible for that?'

She shook her head. 'Unfortunately, this was the result of my own carelessness. Or maybe a farmer's negligence, but I suppose I had no right to climb over his gate, whether it was rickety or not.' She went on to explain what had happened, feeling more at ease in the stranger's company than in Leo's.

'So, for more reasons than one,' Nathan said slowly, 'Leo's taken pity on another of Jerome's casualties. Only this time he's not only had to——'

He hesitated, finding his fingernails unexpectedly interesting.

'Taken pity.' Rhea noted Nathan's words. She wouldn't have associated Leo Dower with any form of sentiment, not even such an easily provoked emotion as pity. Anyone who mismanages their lives, she could hear him saying almost as if he were present, as she had seemed to mismanage hers, deserved what they got.

She took Nathan up. 'Not only had to pay me off— that's what you were going to say, wasn't it?—but also had to put me up, or put up with me, whichever you prefer, for the duration of my immobility?'

He ran his hand lightly over the dark polished wood of the high chairback. 'You sound like one hell of a sore and disappointed person. The others, Leo said, didn't seem to care a damn, just as long as he was prepared to help them out of their predicament. Every one of them was intending, they told him, to rid themselves of the consequences of their actions. All in a day's work for them, he reckoned. Which, Leo being the kind of man he is, infuriated him.'

What kind of man? she was going to ask, but her embittered mind suppressed the question. She didn't want to know anything about Leo Dower as a person. He meant nothing to her, nor would he ever.

There had been genuine concern in Nathan's voice, and Rhea felt herself warming to him. Leo's friend he might be, she thought, but his surname was not Dower, and that made all the difference.

'I'm more than sore and disappointed, Mr Oxley, much, much more,' she told him.

'Do you think you could call me Nathan, since it seems you're likely to be here for a while yet?'

'If you like. And I'm Rhea.'

He smiled. 'Rhea. The others,' he continued with his theme, 'were, or so Leo said, hard-bitten bi—— Sorry, *ladies.*'

'Does Leo know you're here?' she asked, partly to change the subject.

He nodded. 'I popped into the forge during a break from my work. He told me that if I paid a visit to his cottage I'd find another surprise package that had been delivered to his doorstep, courtesy of Jerome. Sorry,' as he noted her heightened colour, 'to be going on about that subject. He actually asked if I'd mind making sure you were OK.'

'A caring Dower? I just don't believe it.'

'Yes, well ... I can understand your feelings, but including Leo in your low opinion of that family...' Nathan shook his head. 'When you get to know him better——'

'That's something I don't intend to do, Nathan.'

'Pity.' His shoulders lifted and fell. 'He's a great guy, and a superb craftsman.'

'Does he work for his uncle?' she asked, then reproached herself for showing even a passing interest in the man.

'*With* his uncle—a subtle difference. Timmy Dower's a good old-fashioned blacksmith. Leo's alter ego's a businessman.'

'You mean he's taking time off from his real work?'

Nathan nodded. 'He believes that a man's—not to mention a woman's—inner needs are as important as his—or her—material needs. So now and then he says to hell with the pursuit of wealth and position and takes a few months off to refresh his spirit.' Nathan glanced at her. 'Didn't you know any of this? Didn't Jerome tell you?'

'He hardly ever talked about his brother,' Rhea answered slowly, 'except on one occasion when he gave a none-too-tasty character reference.'

Nathan smiled and after a small pause asked, 'Are you in pain?' He nodded towards her foot.

'Yes, but I try not to think about it. I wish I hadn't been so stupid as to cause it to happen. I wouldn't be here now...'

'Hey,' Nathan glanced at the carriage clock on the mantelpiece, 'it's coffee time.'

Rhea made to rise. 'I'll get it——'

'Oh, no, you won't,' Nathan joked, getting to his feet. 'I'd know my way round this place blindfold, so I'll do the honours.'

'What's your line?' Rhea asked as they sipped coffee and nibbled biscuits.

'I'm a potter. You must come and see my place some time. That is, if you could see it—my house, I mean—for the chaos I live and work in.'

Rhea smiled. 'Doesn't your wife complain?'

Nathan studied his hands. 'My wife upped and left. I'm currently partnerless.' Subject closed.

Rhea sensed that he didn't even want her to offer sympathy. 'Pottery,' she said instead, 'the making of it, has always fascinated me——'

'Cosy twosome,' said Leo from the doorway, giving Rhea a fright, but not startling Nathan in the least.

'Talk of the devil,' Nathan said.

'Which you weren't,' Leo remarked, strolling in, hands in pockets, his solid frame encased again in black T-shirt and dark, workworn trousers. 'I heard the conversation from the invitation to visit your place onwards.' He looked inscrutably from Rhea to his friend.

Nathan smiled. 'Want to make something of it, pal?'

'Not if the lady doesn't.' His glance brought the colour rushing to Rhea's cheeks. Not only was his look overtly sensual, but he was insulting her by assuming that be-

cause she had been Jerome's girlfriend she was the type
to run after any man.

As he moved nearer, Rhea grew annoyed with her heart
which insisted on trying to run the two-minute mile. This
man, she tried telling it, means nothing to me...or you.
Understand? But it continued to ignore her sharp
reprimand.

'Would you like some coffee, Mr Dower?' she asked,
her tone as matter-of-fact as she could make it.

He reached out and fitted his hand threateningly round
her neck, tilting her head back. She felt herself shiver
alarmingly, trying to suppress the tingle that ran up and
down her spine. 'L-e-o, Leo,' he spelt out. His clasp
tightened. 'Say it.'

'Leo.' It came from her chokily, her eyes fighting his.
It was Nathan's turn then to look from one to the other.

'I've already discovered, Leo,' he remarked, 'that your
guest seems to bear an enormous grudge against the
Dowers. You must find it refreshing to discover a lady
who isn't chucking herself at your feet.'

'Only to be trodden on in the true Dower tradition?'
Rhea queried with an over-sweet smile.

'I,' said Nathan, draining his cup and rising, 'had
better be making myself scarce. A war seems about to
break out between you two, and I'd hate to get caught
in the crossfire.' He left, saying he had enjoyed meeting
Leo's 'surprise package', and repeated his invitation to
Rhea to visit his place some time.

Pouring coffee, Leo turned to Rhea, eyeing her dis-
concertingly over the rim of his cup. Her disobedient
gaze strayed, contemplating the well-formed arm
muscles, the layer of dark hair from his wrists upwards,
the way the T-shirt moulded to his solid frame.

Then she told her eyes to stop being swept towards
the whirlpool, because, if they didn't, she would surely
drown there. Couldn't they, she asked them, see the word
'Danger' flung across the dark vortex that was his

physique, his ambience, his entire personality, drawing her ever closer?

'You were getting on well with Nathan Oxley.'

His voice was edged and her eyes sparked defiantly.

'Better than with you, you mean? *He* seems a very easy person to get on with.'

He ignored her provocative emphasis. 'Added to which, of course, you don't possess this grudge against him that you've got against the name Dower?'

'The *two brothers* named Dower,' she threw back, the rancour in her own voice surprising even herself. 'Jerome and——' Some strange restraint held her back from completing the sentence.

'Leo?' He seemed unduly annoyed. He crossed to stand in front of her. 'What the hell have I ever done to you?'

'Just—just being Jerome's brother is enough.'

'How can an apparently well-balanced woman get so prejudiced?'

'He told me things about you, like...' Dared she? 'You were——' Once again something made her hesitate.

'I was——?' His eyebrows arched, his lips twisted. 'Go on.'

'You cared nothing for others, particularly women. You took life as it came, kind of shrugging it off. You were as hard as granite and used every experience—women, Jerome said he meant—to the full, then put it—them—behind you and moved on to the next, and the next...'

'Wow!' It was a long-drawn-out, sarcastic sound. He drained his cup and clattered it down, anger in the gesture, but there was only a silky rebuke in his voice as he commented, 'Has he given me a glowing testimonial! A truly brotherly one. Have I so far, in your opinion, lived up to my callous reputation?'

No, a voice whispered. Rhea looked down, moving her injured leg, then wishing she hadn't. 'I—I don't know

you well enough yet, do I, to answer that question? And,'
she challenged him, 'I don't intend to hang around here
long enough to find out.'

He found a footstool, lifting her leg on to it, pushing
another cushion behind her back for better support.
Startled, she stared up at him.

'Uncaring, eh? Self-orientated? Others can go to hell,'
he stood in front of her again, hands on hips, 'when
I've finished with them?'

She frowned up at him. '*I* didn't say that. It was your
brother.'

'Nevertheless, you believe it.'

She looked away. 'Thank you for your thought-
fulness. But please, don't go overboard in trying to please
me just to prove that your brother's opinion of you is
wrong.'

'I could,' his eyes narrowed dangerously, 'take exception to your colossal impudence.'

'OK, so throw me out. I'll manage to cope. I've had
problems to overcome in the recent past that were much
more difficult than merely having to incorporate a leg
in a cast into my daily life.' Her voice rang with defiance, her eyes carrying on the fight.

Leo considered her, his expression unreadable, ap-
pearing in the end to let her challenge go.

'So,' he said slowly, 'no acquittal for the Dowers? No
reassessment of your prejudiced judgement of them?'

'No. But there's no *prejudice* involved, only brutal
facts to back it up. And please don't try and plead your
brother's cause. You don't know what he... You just
don't know.'

'Rhea, look at me.' She forcibly suppressed the shiver
that took hold at the piercing gaze that met hers. 'Did
he force you to lose the child?'

It actually seemed to matter to him! 'Of course not,'
she returned, 'how could he, when there was no——?'
Child, she had been about to say, when he broke in,

'Of course,' with an inexplicable bitterness, 'no force was necessary because there was never any need, with big brother Leo's bank balance always there to come to his—and his assorted girlfriends'—rescue.'

The rear entrance door opened and a short, grey-haired man in an overall and tweed cap stepped in, nodding and smiling with great affability. He removed the cap, stuffing it into a pocket.

Didn't he know, Rhea pondered, wondering at his warmth and apparent acceptance of her, who she was? Hadn't he heard about the low status that had been conferred on her by Leo Dower as merely one of his brother's throw-away women?

—'Rhea Hirst, Timmy, my uncle,' said Leo, his careless sweeping gesture concluding the casual introduction, 'my father's brother. Beware of the lady, Timmy. She snarls and bites anyone with the name Dower.'

'No, I don't,' Rhea exclaimed, taking an instant liking to the newcomer. 'Not everyone.'

There was, she noticed, a family likeness, a faint look of Jerome about him; a trace of Leo too, although the older man's face was creased with sympathy lines, which meant that the comparison ended there. Leo's character contained not an atom of sympathy—hadn't she been warned, and hadn't she seen it for herself? Also, Timmy Dower lacked his elder nephew's hard resolution, the rocklike determination that flared in Leo's eyes. 'I'm very selective,' she added, 'in the people I put on my hate list.'

Timmy chuckled loudly, his pale eyes seeking those of his nephew. 'She's either an impudent baggage, this young lady, Leo, or she's got real guts, to pit herself against you.'

'I think the latter, Mr Dower.' Timmy waved Rhea's formality away. 'Timmy,' she amended. 'Because *they* have been well and truly tried in the last few months.'

She flashed Leo a belligerent look. 'I don't think they were found wanting.'

'It's plain Rhea knows her own worth, lad,' Timmy said, easing his small frame on to the chair Nathan had recently vacated.

'I wasn't meaning to boast, Timmy,' Rhea explained, 'but in the past few months I've really and truly had to come face to face not just with life, but with myself. I had to trust someone, and since there was no one else I could turn to I just had to trust me.'

'Leo's told me about you, lass,' Timmy said soberly. 'About your accident. About you and Jerome...'

That hadn't been what she had meant, but she did not correct him.

'It's shocking, Leo,' Timmy was saying, 'the way Jerome plays around, messing up young women's lives. Crazy,' he scratched his head, 'the way they let him. And to think of the little mites he——'

'Procreates and runs away from, yes,' Leo broke in grimly. 'If I knew where the little s——' he glanced at Rhea, then continued '—beggar was, I'd wring his neck, then I'd give him an ultimatum. Marry the latest mother-to-be of your child, or I'll throw you off my list of charities.'

'For heaven's sake,' Rhea's voice hit a high note, 'I wouldn't want to marry him. I hate him now, *hate him*!'

To her horror, she burst into tears, her shoulders shaking with sobs. She hadn't the slightest idea why it had happened. She had no feelings left for Jerome Dower. The sofa cushion beside her gave and an unfamiliar arm went round her shoulders.

'There, there,' an understanding voice said, 'don't cry like that, lass. I expect you're in pain with your ankle?' She nodded. 'Well, everything'll turn out right, you'll see. Leo will make sure of that. It's too bad, Leo, what Jerome's done.' The shocked voice quavered. 'Isn't there any way of tracing him?'

'I don't want him traced!' Rhea exclaimed through her tears. 'I don't care if I never see him again. All I want is my car and the personal belongings I'd packed in it. Jerome can go to——'

'Uncle, let me...' An exchange was made, a bigger, bulkier figure positioned itself beside her. 'We understand your reaction, Rhea, the resentment you feel at Jerome's treatment after all there's been between you. And you were his fiancée, for God's sake.'

There was a gasp of surprise from the older man. 'You mean he'd even proposed marriage, then went off just like that?'

'He's let me down,' Rhea's voice emerged thickly from between her hands, 'as no one in the whole world has ever let me down before.'

An arm came round her whose potential strength sent urgent messages to her reflexes to give in to her instincts and succumb to the reassurance and security it offered. She was urged sideways, and she didn't resist. Her heated forehead found a hard, broad sanctuary beneath which was a pounding drum similar in noise and rhythm to the hammering that had greeted her as she had walked down the village street the day before.

A wide-spanning hand rubbed up and down her back in a gesture similar to that of a mother—or a father—comforting a child. Her reaction to the comforter's touch was, to her dismay, anything but childish. Her reflexes jumped to life, her skin seemed to shiver and tingle, and her eyes, which had been closed, came open.

Her head eased back and she gazed into the piercing gaze that had brought her limbs and, almost, her heart, to a stop the first time she had met and locked with it.

She searched those eyes, watching as a momentary shaft of sensual light overrode the detached concern. Then it had gone, but it had left her senses reeling. And her heart afraid. She mustn't, she told herself, *she must not* let either herself or her emotions become entangled in the invisible, dangerous net that billowed around this man.

Intuition told her that, if she were ever to be so foolish, there would be no way out, she would be caught for ever, because from a man like this there would be no merciful hand throwing her back into the sea, into the outside world.

His jaw had ridged under her seeking gaze, his arm muscles had tensed and she sensed that for some reason he was angry, and with her too. She separated herself from him and he leaned back, arms folded, expression grim.

'There's not much resemblance, is there,' Timmy broke into the brittle silence, 'between him and his brother? I expect that was what you were looking for, dear.' There was sympathy in his tone. 'The nose, maybe, the eyes——'

'Not the eyes!' The words burst from her, surprising her listeners and even herself with their vehemence. 'Same colour,' Rhea remarked more calmly, 'but——' How could she explain? 'Jerome's aren't so—so forceful, so analytical, so...' Exciting, electrifying, *inviting*... She couldn't say those words aloud, so she lifted her shoulders as if lost for words. 'So cold,' she finished, with a daring glance at Leo.

Timmy laughed. 'She's got you taped, lad,' he commented. 'All fact and no fantasy, all brain and no heart, that's what others say about him.'

But *I* know, Rhea thought, that underneath that stony, impassive exterior, something—a spark, a smouldering ember—exists that, given the right circumstances, could fire a woman's femininity to ardent, eager life. Hadn't others noticed? Surely his women friends had glimpsed what she had sensed...no, *seen*?

But then a man who held himself as aloof from emotion, from any depth of feeling, as it was perfectly obvious Leo Dower did, would surely take his lovers coldly and clinically, no matter how warmly and fervently they might respond to his lovemaking?

'Thanks, Timmy,' Leo said sarcastically, 'for confirming in our guest's mind everything she's been told about me by my dear brother. Got your sandwiches?'

Timmy reached into the pocket of the dusty jacket he had hung over the chair back, pulling out a packet.

'Cheese and pickle,' he informed then. 'They always are. I made them myself, as usual.' He sighed. 'I miss your auntie's clever hand with fillings, Leo. I miss her more than anyone will ever know.' A long pause, then, pulling himself out of his unhappiness, 'Where are the cans of beer, lad?'

Leo disappeared to the kitchen.

'I lost my wife,' Timmy told Rhea, peeling the wrapper from the sandwiches, 'a year ago.' He crumpled the paper. 'We're a close family, the Dowers—what's left of us,' he added, tearing off a chunk of sandwich and chewing it reflectively. 'Leo's mother died when he was ten. His father brought in another woman, name of Andrea, then eventually married her. She and Leo—they never hit it off, and she never seemed to take to Jerome either.'

Rhea listened, half of her not wanting to because there must be no softening of her attitude towards the Dower brothers, the other half so interested that she could hardly wait for Timmy to continue.

'Which meant,' Timmy went on between mouthfuls, 'that Leo turned protective towards his brother and shielded him from the harsh words meted out to them both by their stepmother. Their father, Horrie—Horace, short for——' Rhea nodded '—never seemed to notice, he was so wrapped up in his work. Ran the Dower steel fabrication business.'

Even Rhea had heard of the Dower Corporation and, since the name could hardly be called a particularly common one, could not understand why she had not connected the two brothers with it.

'So Leo and Jerome have always been close,' Timmy concluded. 'You understand, lass?'

Again Rhea nodded. It explained a lot of things. 'Jerome never told me anything about his background,' she remarked.

'He wouldn't, would he? Not to a young lady he never intended——'

'But we were engaged!' Rhea exclaimed.

Timmy shook his head. 'It might have meant a lot to you, Rhea. It didn't mean anything to Jerome, I can tell you that, fond uncle though I am.'

'Does Leo's father still——?'

'Run the Dower Corporation?' He shook his head, dusting the crumbs from his clothes. 'In name, maybe, but he b——' he cleared his throat, glancing sideways at Rhea '—he buzzed off to the Bahamas with his second wife. He leaves it all to Leo now. Who leaves it to his deputy when the urge comes upon him to throw it all aside for a few months and join me in the forge. It's his first love, the forge—isn't it, Leo? Ah, thanks,' as his nephew handed him a beer from the tray he had carried in. 'What about the lady?'

'No alcohol for her. Fruit juice,' said Leo decisively, and gave Rhea a prepared drink. Rhea guessed the reason at once. Let him think whatever he likes, she thought with a mental shrug. In two or three weeks she'd be leaving and he need never know the truth.

While Timmy demolished an apple, Rhea watched as Leo sliced hunks of bread from a long French loaf. He added a chunk of cheese, then quirked an eyebrow and asked, 'Rhea, you like? Yes?'

Shaking pieces of washed lettuce from a dish, he placed them on her plate, adding a whole tomato, then hesitated as he reached with a spoon for a small brown onion. He looked at her, his brows arched in query.

'I—well, I——'

'If you're worried about the residual aroma,' he said, to the accompaniment of Timmy's deep chuckle, 'don't be.'

'Well, if you're having one...' Then she stopped, colouring deeply. She had strayed into forbidden territory, and he took her up with a sardonic smile.

'Rest assured,' he remarked, 'there's no way I'll be kissing you today. Nor you me. OK?'

Rhea nodded, blushing, annoyed at the way her fair skin always let the world know her feelings. And why, she asked her heart desperately, do you have to hammer as fast as a woodpecker at a tree-trunk?

'I've been telling this young lady a thing or two about you,' Timmy announced to his nephew. 'Put her in the picture—that's what they call it nowadays, isn't it? Seeing as how she's going to produce the next generation of Dowers.' The crunch of his apple sounded loud in the difficult silence. 'You and Jerome—inseparable, you were. Which is why Jerome's always running to his brother for help. Isn't that so, Leo?'

'Is it?' Leo answered flatly, bringing an end to his uncle's revelations.

'Is this,' Rhea ventured later over the coffee which Leo had made, 'your usual lunchtime routine? You eat here——?'

Timmy shook his head. 'We go to the Dog and Badger most days, don't we, Leo? Meet our pals there. We came back here today to keep you company—Leo's idea.'

'That was very nice of you both, and I've enjoyed it,' offered Rhea, 'but please don't worry about me in future.'

'Think nothing of it, lass. Would you,' Timmy looked at her doubtfully, 'would you come with us sometimes?'

'To the Dog and Badger? I'd love to.'

'She sounds as though she means it, Leo,' said Timmy, going to wash his hands.

'It's something I never did with Jerome,' she said slowly, as Leo cleared the debris.

'Have a ploughman's lunch or go to a pub?'

'Both. It was always the best restaurants. He never seemed to tire of the formality, the slightly exotic food that some of them serve, the subservient waiters. I tried telling him I'd like to go somewhere else, but——'

'Jerome loves playing the wealthy tycoon,' was Leo's brotherly comment, 'even though his intellectual powers could never raise him up to that standard. Where did you meet him?' Hands in his pockets, he slanted a glance down at her as she reclined lengthways on the sofa, both legs resting.

'At one of those "best" restaurants.' She smiled faintly at the irony. 'At the bar. I was with my parents. We'd gone there for a celebration meal. It was my mother's birthday—her fiftieth.' Rhea paused because it pained her to remember that her mother had seen only one more birthday after that.

'So Jerome got talking?' Leo prompted. 'He usually does.'

'To my father, yes.'

'With his eye on you. And you returned his interest, giving him come-on signals?'

'No, I didn't. I——'

'Oh, come on, Rhea! You must have given him some encouragement. He asked you out, and you went? Which is how it all began, yes? I know by heart Jerome's routine in his pursuit of the opposite sex.'

Timmy returned, pulling on his jacket. 'I'll be off, Leo. See you again, lass.' He smiled in a kindly way. 'I can tell you've got more pain from that foot than you let on about. No hurry, Leo. Take your time.'

'Is it hurting?' asked Leo. 'Why didn't you say?' He produced the bottle of painkillers, but Rhea shook her head.

As the door closed on Timmy, there was a heavy silence. 'There was more to it than that,' she said slowly. 'My father was head of a big company, an up-market clothing chain.'

'Daniel Hirst?' Leo queried with some surprise. 'I've bought their clothes myself in the past. Couldn't discover what happened to the firm.'

'They were bought up,' Rhea answered heavily. 'It was the name the buyers were after. The company itself was hardly worth anything. It was on the verge of collapsing even before my father's death, though I didn't know that at the time.'

'So?' He dropped into an armchair, seeming impatient with her silence.

'Jerome made such an impression on my father at that first meeting that he offered him a job—general manager. Jerome jumped at it.'

'I can imagine,' said his brother drily. 'He told me something about his future father-in-law giving him a plum job.'

Rhea nodded. 'We became engaged very quickly. About two months later, in fact. Then, seeing him—and trusting him—as his future son-in-law, about which Jerome did nothing to discourage his expectations, Dad promoted him.'

'You fell in love with my brother?' Leo's face, like his tone, was expressionless.

'Is it surprising if I did? Good-looking, charming...loving. Told me I meant the world to him. Bought me presents.'

'I can understand your bitterness, Rhea, but women by the dozen have fallen for his wiles. I would have thought,' Leo said reflectively, 'that an intelligent girl like you——'

'Intelligence doesn't come into it,' she returned sharply. 'But you wouldn't know, would you, with your cool and clinical approach to all matters affecting the heart. Heart to you,' she realised she was speaking too fiercely, 'means this,' she touched her chest with her fist, 'something that keeps a human being alive, nothing to do with emotions, feelings...'

'OK, you hate me.' He shrugged and rose. 'I'll relieve you of my obnoxious company. In an emergency, you can always ring me at this number.' He found a telephone pad and scribbled on it, handing it to her. 'It's the forge.' With that, he was gone.

The room, which had seemed so cosy, seemed to ring with the emptiness he had left behind. Rhea told herself firmly to stop being so stupid. She wasn't really missing his vital presence. Because of her incapacity, she had grown dependent on him, on his latent strength, on the reassurance his presence offered.

There couldn't possibly be any other reason. Could there?

CHAPTER FOUR

LATER, Leo rang, startling her. Rhea almost dropped the phone as she picked it up.

'Leo Dower's house.'

'Is it, now? Whadderyouknow!' Rhea visualised Leo's tantalising solidity leaning indolently against some support, his strong mouth curved sardonically. 'Seems I've got myself a real live answering machine.'

'What do you want?' she asked, annoyed because at the sound of his voice her heart had done its usual ballet-dancer's leap.

'Could you feed yourself this evening? I've got a date.'

Why did her heart jolt now like a car doing a crash stop? 'Yes, I could. Thank you for calling.'

His sarcastic laughter rang in her ears long after he had gone. It was a long evening. She took some cold meat from the fridge and made a salad, hopping around and holding on to the modern kitchen units. She wriggled on to a high stool and ate sideways on at the breakfast bar, her leg propped stiffly on the footrest.

Using one of the crutches, she managed to wash the dishes, finding the dishwasher too awkward to cope with in her present state. For an hour or two she watched television, then, aware of a general feeling of discomfort, she decided to attempt a shower.

The nurse at the hospital had said that, if she was careful, this was permissible because the leg cast, being made of a water-repellent material, would stand up to a wetting provided she didn't allow the water to trickle down through the gap at the top.

There was a shower over the bath, with curtains fixed to slide all round the bathtub, which pleased her, just in case Leo arrived back early and came to seek her out. Although there was no way, she was certain, that he would tear himself from the arms of his beloved Sonya until the early hours at least, if then.

Securing her nightclothes under her arms, she hopped painfully with the crutches into the bathroom. Getting into the bath was easier than she had thought. A conveniently placed soapdish became a useful item to hold on to. She had never had a one-footed shower before. It proved quite difficult, but as she reached to turn the shower off she rejoiced in the resulting feeling of cleanliness.

Turning, standing on her good foot, she faced the problem of getting out of the bath. She bent down to rest her hand on the side, intending to seat herself on it, reversing the process of getting in, but she had not reckoned with the slipperiness of the shower gel still clinging to her skin through hurried and insufficient rinsing.

To her horror, she felt her foot slipping slowly along the base of the bath, and, unable to save herself, she landed with a bump that jarred her spine. She tried in vain to get up, looking round helplessly and wishing she had never attempted to have the shower unaided and unsupervised.

Then her reason told her that even if Leo had been there she wouldn't have allowed him into the bathroom to help her, not under any circumstances. Now she would have to make the best of it and stay there, all night if necessary, until help arrived. That it might well come in the form of a hunk of a man with powerful arms and a lashing tongue she hardly dared to contemplate.

Seizing her sponge-bag, which she had placed, together with the towel, within easy reach, she lowered herself until she was lying flat, elbowing the sponge-bag so that it acted as a pillow. She spread the towel over her, wishing as she did so that the sun's warmth had lingered longer. She must, she thought, have drifted off, since she was jerked back to consciousness by the sound of a car half skidding to a stop.

The entrance door was flung open and she started to shiver. There was a pause, the proverbial calm before the storm. Footsteps pounded the stairs, then came the explosion.

'Rhea, where in *hell's name* are you?' In two seconds he was in the bathroom, dragging aside the shower curtains and staring down at her. He had blanched and his breath came in short, angry bursts. 'My God, I thought you'd——'

'Gone? Or,' she suggested, trying a smile but discovering that her mouth was shivering too, 'got so desperate I tried to——?' She shook her head slowly, except that it juddered at the movement. 'I've already told you, I'm not like that. I face my problems—and solve them.'

'So,' colour normal now, hands on hips, his anger having been overtaken by ironic amusement, 'how did you intend solving this little problem?' His eyes were travelling the length of her as though she were an interesting and rare species of *Homo sapiens* that might be reported to be nearest anthropological society. He actually seemed to be enjoying it.

The towel had slipped to one side and, damp though it now was, she grabbed it and tried to cover her vital parts. But she couldn't stop shivering. She was tired and cold, and, in her present plight, the injured foot was showing no mercy, turning on a nagging pain.

Leo left the bathroom and she thought he had walked out on her. Forgetting her promise to herself that she wouldn't even allow him into the room, she cried out,

'Please, Leo, don't leave me like this! I'm c-cold and t-tired and——'

He returned, his smile taunting, in his hands a fresh, dry towel. 'Can't do without the Dowers, can you?' he mocked, looking down at her again and missing nothing of her curves and mounds and other physical attractions. 'Hate them though you do, you've got to admit they have their uses.' He still made no move to remove her from the bathtub. 'She's at my mercy.' The words rumbled around his chest. 'What condition shall I impose for getting her out of her predicament?'

'None, Leo.' She stared up at him, eyes wide, teeth chattering. 'I'm not—I don't—I can't.' I know what he'll think, she told herself frantically, but I don't care.

'OK, message received.' His expression tightened. He seemed angry again. He gave her the towel, which she wrapped around herself as best she could. Then those arms scooped her up and held her against him, the leg imprisoned in plaster protruding at an awkward angle. She gave a great sneeze, her body jarring with it.

It was late, and her rescuer's jaw was dark with stubble shadow. Rhea felt the totally forbidden urge to run the back of her fingers over it. That urge had come from nowhere, and she told it that that was where it must return.

Beside her bed Leo let her down, threading her carefully through his hands. Rhea was thankful that the towel was around her. Nevertheless, the pressure of his palms in over-sensitive places made her skin prickle beneath the shiver that still had her teeth chattering.

Without warning her of their intention, her arms lifted to cling to his solid frame. Her body started shaking again, almost out of control. His enveloping arms pulled her to him, and the warmth of him flooded through her, steadying the trembling that frightened in its intensity. Her head bumped against his shoulder, her fingers grasping upper arms that were rock-hard beneath the cotton shirt he wore.

'S-sorry about this,' she managed, compressing her quivering lips.

He tipped her chin, looking at her keenly. 'What's wrong?'

'C-cold.' Her tired amber eyes stared worriedly up at the face that was becoming alarmingly familiar, and not only because it bore minute traces of Jerome. 'I c-can't stop shivering.'

Lips tight, almost forbidding, he helped her slide her nightdress down her body, his touch, like his glance, coolly impersonal. Then he folded the covers down, turned her so that she sank on to the bed and lifted her legs, easing the covers over her as she reclined against the pillows.

'Five minutes.'

He took three, giving her a cup of hot milk and seating himself, arms folded, on the bed while she drank it. 'How's the injury?' he asked.

'Making itself felt.' Shivers banished at last, she found she could speak without stammering.

'Tablets?' Reluctantly Rhea nodded. Counting out two, he pushed the bottle back into his trouser pocket. 'Just what the doctor ordered.'

'There's no need,' she protested, 'to dole them out. I told you——'

'This Dower is taking no chances where the next generation's concerned.'

She closed her lips over the denial that sprang every time Leo made the false assumption that the 'next generation' of Dowers was on the way. Anyway, if she told him the truth before her mobility returned, he might throw her out, and she needed his help too much at the moment to risk that.

As soon as the plaster was off, as soon as she could walk normally again, she would be gone. She couldn't stay here any longer. Something was happening to her emotions. Every time the man she told herself she hated came into view, they behaved crazily. Every time, even, that she thought about him . . . Like the teeth-chattering shock that had been so frightening in the way it seemed to have taken hold of her, so the thought of her emotions getting beyond her control worried her immensely.

When she left this house, that problem would be solved. The Dower family would be left behind, going out of her thoughts and out of her life. Forever.

Gritting her teeth four days later, Rhea made her slow way over the bridge and along the road to the forge. She had seen very little of Leo since he had rescued her from the bath. He had left for work by the time she had struggled down to breakfast. He had not returned for the evening meal, staying out late, she presumed, to get away from her.

Well, she told herself acidly, his dislike of her was heartily reciprocated. He was Jerome's brother, and that was enough to make her hate him for life.

Over the ringing of the anvil and the striking of the hammer came the sound of voices. A woman's laughter mixed in with a man's deeper laughing note, jokes striking sparks, words tossed between friends, meaning nothing to an outsider.

Which was exactly how Rhea felt as, supported by her crutches, she stood at the door gazing into the semi-darkness. The fire cast flickering shadows all around. She was hot and tired with the concentrated, teeth-gritting effort that the walk from Leo's cottage had demanded.

Lounging back against a wooden table, Leo stiffened, a can of beer halfway to his mouth. His female companion was seated, legs drawn up gnome-like, on a battered stool.

'What the hell are you doing here?' Leo asked, lowering the can and straightening. 'You're supposed to be resting with your feet up.'

So he's annoyed with me for spoiling his tête-à-tête with his girlfriend. 'I got bored,' she told him, 'and anyway, I needed the exercise.'

'Sonya,' Leo sketched a brisk introduction, 'Rhea Hirst. Rhea, Sonya Selby.'

'So, Leo,' said the lady, unfolding her legs and inspecting Rhea as if she were of a different species, 'this is the "Jerome cast-off" you were telling me about?' Slowly, encased shoulder to ankle in a fluorescent pink outfit that emphasised the dimness of the interior, Sonya approached. 'What a clever girl you are,' she remarked, eyeing Rhea from top to toe, 'to have outdone your fellow sufferers and discovered a way they never thought of, of getting Leo to accommodate you not just financially but physically.'

In the background, the coke fire spat and crackled like Rhea's anger. 'If you think, Miss—Mrs?—Selby, that I deliberately injured myself so as to play on Mr Dower's sympathies——' She switched her fiery gaze to Leo. 'Is that what you think too? That I fell off that farm gate and broke some bones to force you to take me in?'

Leo took a drink, head slightly back, eyes watchful.

Goaded by his silence, Rhea flung at him, 'No answer, which means that you do.' She made to swing round, but a crutch settled on a stray piece of iron on the floor and started to unbalance her. Leo was there, catching her by the shoulders, steadying her.

She twisted out of his hold, lifting burning eyes to his. She had had her fill of his touch the other evening when he had rescued her from the bath. She couldn't stand what it did to her, the way it played on her senses and lingered in her mind. 'Will you tell me, please, where Nathan Oxley lives?' she asked him.

'Down in the village.' Leo's eyes narrowed. 'Why?'

'To seduce him, that's why!' she retorted.

Sonya's laugh rang out. For a few frightening seconds, a lightning-strike of fury flickered across Leo's eyes.

'You don't really think I meant——?' Rhea choked, then, Yes, he does, she thought, he thinks exactly the same of me as he did of those 'others' they all talk about. Well, let him!

She added more calmly, 'He invited me to call on him any time. I'd like to see his work. Any objections, *Mr Dower*?' She knew she would anger him by using his surname, but she didn't care. Two against one, she thought, looking from one to the other, wasn't fair, but she'd hold her own come what may.

'His place is about half a mile on from here,' Sonya told her, plainly anxious to be rid of the irritating outsider. 'On the left as you enter the village.'

Into two mugs she poured tea from a large pot. Rhea noted that she had not been invited to join them and accepted the snub with a mental shrug, consoling herself with the thought that every day that passed brought her nearer to release from the leg cast and her exit from these two people's lives.

'I'll drive you,' said Leo, going to the door.

'Thanks, but no. As I said, I need the exercise.' With a saccharine-sweet smile, she bade goodbye to his lady friend.

Her instincts, too finely tuned where he was concerned, told her that he stood watching as she moved with painful slowness along the road. When, after a few moments, she paused for breath, she turned, hoping he was still there. At that moment she would have given anything for the lift he had offered, but he had gone.

The morning sun shone warmly as, a short while later, she paused again, wondering if she could make it to Nathan's. A car approached slowly and she stood to one side of the narrow country road.

The vehicle stopped and the driver wound down the window. 'Hi, there, Rhea,' said Nathan. 'Just got a phone call from Leo. "One temporarily disabled lady is on her way to pay you a visit," he said. "For heaven's sake, go and meet her. She's making such slow progress it's painful to watch her."'

'I'm surprised,' Rhea commented, thankfully easing herself with Nathan's help on to the rear seat, 'that I touch any part of Leo Dower's feelings, but I'm sure he resents my presence so much, "pain"—as "in the neck"—would, I suppose, be the one word he'd associate with me!'

'Don't you believe it,' remarked Nathan good humouredly. 'Any unattached male would be glad to have someone as decorative and attractive as you in his house, even for a few weeks.'

'Attractive? Using crutches?'

Nathan's glance moved momentarily to the driving-mirror as Rhea shook her head, then stifled a sigh. 'You just don't know, Nathan. I hope,' she went on, changing the subject, 'you don't mind my taking you up on your invitation to visit you.'

'Delighted,' he said, driving along the village street and turning into a parking area adjoining a grey stone cottage bounded by an equally grey stone wall.

The entrance door led into a living-room which, she noted, was welcomingly, although somewhat shabbily, furnished. Nor could it be called tidy. Was this what Nathan's wife had run from, she wondered, chaos such as this which so often went with creativeness and artistic ability? Or had something deeper and more serious undermined their relationship?

Making sure she was comfortable, Nathan made some tea, generally trying to make her feel at home. She found that surprisingly easy, experiencing none of the awkwardness and restraint that tied her feelings into knots in Leo's house. Here, she felt she was welcome. There, she knew she was not.

Nathan took her into his studio. Tables and shelves were covered with partly finished work. Here again there was a general air of untidiness. To one side stood a stool pulled up to a solid-looking table bearing a potter's wheel, hand tools, pots of varying sizes holding coloured liquids and powdered chemicals and, close by, a pair of clay-caked rubber gloves.

'My kiln,' said Nathan, pointing across the room. He opened its door, revealing the pieces awaiting firing. In a display cabinet were finished products, table-lamps and vases, dishes and ornaments, children's night lamps—hollow earthenware tree-trunks with tiny animals peeping from holes.

'There are different types of pottery,' he explained, 'depending on the clay used and the temperatures at which the articles are fired.'

Rhea nodded. 'Such as earthenware, stoneware, porcelain.'

'You know?'

'Mm.' She pointed to the brilliant colours he had used on some of his work. 'Your designs—they're really attractive,' she commented. 'Do you, like me, get them from nature, or do they come out of your head?'

'They're not my work. My—er—wife added those.' A short pause, then, 'It's over, Rhea, whatever others might say. I've no regrets. Well, very few.' Nathan looked at her. 'You said something just now that puzzled me. About the source of these designs.'

Colouring a little, she played back her own words. *Like me,* she'd said.

'There's an awful lot you're not telling us, isn't there,' he remarked, his interest apparent, 'about Rhea Hirst's abilities?'

They were in the living-room again, Rhea seated on a settee with her injured leg on a footstool. What should she tell him? The truth? She felt she owed it to him since, of the people she had so far met, he had been the most pleasant and friendly.

She opted instead for the partial truth. 'I can embroider and weave.'

'Ah—hobbies.' He smiled, satisfied with his own explanation. 'You've probably read craft books?'

'Yes, I have.' That at least was true.

He drew some volumes from his packed shelves. 'While I brew some more tea, have a look at those. We've got a craft group going in the village. You might like to come along some time.'

Rhea smiled, her eyes still on the colourful pages. 'I certainly would,' she raised her voice to reach him in the kitchen, 'but I won't be around here for much longer. The moment I get rid of this leg cast, I'll be on my way.'

'Where to?' He was placing her tea mug on a handy table. 'Or are you going to tell me it's none of my business?'

'No.' She stared at the book, not really seeing it. 'The honest answer is, I don't know.' She closed the book and saw Nathan's concerned frown. 'I'll land on my feet, Nathan, like a cat's always alleged to do.'

'You're no cat, Rhea.' He removed the book, then lifted her hand, inspecting her nails. 'No claws, like the others Jerome Dower played around with, then chucked aside.'

'Thanks.' She spread her hand against the back of his. 'Your hands are large,' she commented with interest.

'A potter's hands.' He turned his palm to hers. 'You need the width and strength to control and form the clay on the potter's wheel.'

'Sorry to break things up,' said a cynical voice from the doorway, 'but I've come for my guest.'

Embarrassed, Nathan detached his hand from Rhea's and faced his visitor.

Leo's hand lifted to rest against the doorframe, disapproval in every line of him. 'A word of advice, pal. If you don't want an interloper to ruin the romance in your life, you shouldn't leave your door on the catch.'

'Come on, Leo,' Nathan protested, 'you've misinterpreted and you damned well know it. I was merely telling Rhea that——'

'Unlike her predecessors, she was clawless. I heard.' Leo's glance sliced down, hitting Rhea, making her shiver. 'Don't you believe it, Nathan. I guess that, being among new acquaintances, she's been on her best behaviour and the claws have been sheathed. She wouldn't want to be thrown out in her state.'

'Don't you mean "condition"?' Rhea asked oversweetly.

His eyelids drooped. 'Don't provoke me—I can get really unpleasant if pushed too far. Nathan will bear witness to that.'

'Leave me out of it, pal. I've got enough troubles of my own. Tea?'

'No, thanks. When my house guest has finished hers, we'll be on our way.'

It was an order, given with a little too much authority for Rhea's liking. Nevertheless, she drained her mug and lowered her leg to the floor. 'Thanks, Nathan, for our interesting chat and for showing me your work.'

He helped her to her feet and handed her the crutches. 'Don't forget my invitation to the group. Did you know, Leo, that your guest was clever with her hands? Her hobbies are embroidery and weaving, she told me. Isn't that right, Rhea?' It was and it wasn't, but Rhea opted for the non-committal course and nodded. 'I've been trying to persuade her to attend our group.'

She was standing now, crutches in place. 'If only I were more mobile...'

'Then you wouldn't be here.' Leo's expression implied so much more than his words conveyed. You'd have gone joyfully on your way like all the others, it said, with a large cheque to pay into your bank account at my expense.

'I can't wait, Mr Dower, to make my getaway,' she dropped acidly into the sudden silence. 'Thanks again, Nathan, for the tea.' To Leo, she added, 'You're waiting to take me home?'

'Home', she heard herself say, and coloured uncomfortably. The last thing she must do, she told herself, was to look upon this man's cottage as her home.

He had noticed her slip, of course, and the mockery in his eyes only increased her confusion. His car was more comfortable than Nathan's, more roomy and smoother-running.

'If you dare to say,' her voice rose over the taped music, 'so you're not just a pretty face, I'll——'

'Thump me? Try, Rhea, try. I retaliate when provoked—in unexpected ways. As my brother has no doubt told you, where conventional behaviour's concerned, I don't run true to form.'

Classical music filled the conversational silence until he broke it with, 'As the daughter of a wealthy man, I guess, you wouldn't have needed to work? Which meant that your hobbies took up most of your time?'

'I gather,' she answered, tight-lipped, 'that you're saying in a roundabout way that educationally I'm a moron?'

'*No,*' he answered with mocking emphasis. 'No doubt finishing-school rounded off your corners and taught you how to cook, how to draw——'

'How to be *clever with my hands*? Just how patronising can you get, Mr Dower? Anyway, I see no reason to tell you anything about myself. Our acquaintance is going to be so short that my abilities, either mental or manual, can be of no concern to you.'

Something inside her erupted. She craved to break away, to get out, escape from the disturbing, disrupting aura of the man beside her. The country quietness outside beckoned and, in itself, offered sanctuary from the destructive force beside her.

'I want to walk,' she got out, her hand on the door catch. 'I'm not staying in this car a moment longer. Let me out, please.' He did not stop, so her wilful hand opened the door.

'For God's sake,' he shouted, stamping on the brake, 'what the hell do you think you're doing?'

'G-getting away—f-from you.' Rhea swung out her good leg, with her hands lifting out the injured one and struggling free of the car's confines. The crutches were on the rear seat, but with one leg out of action she could only stand there.

After a few moments Leo joined her. 'Don't you dare try and put me back in the car!' Rhea cried.

'I wouldn't dream of manhandling a *lady* against her will,' he returned, his emphasis implying that she was the very opposite. He pulled out the crutches and handed them to her one by one.

When she was ready to move, he returned to the car and drove on. He's going to leave me, she thought, furious with herself for having given in to such a foolish impulse. How could she have expected any sympathy, any understanding of her state of mind, from such a man?

To her astonishment, he stopped. When, slowly and painfully, she had caught up with the car, he drove on again, waiting once more, staring ahead, moving a short distance, then halting a third time. His cottage was in view, for a normally mobile person within easy reach, but for her, every step bringing pain with it, a tantalisingly distant goal.

'Please go,' she said through her teeth, determined to show her independence of him. 'I'm OK. I'll manage.'

With a dismissing lift of the shoulder, Leo complied with her request, driving on and disappearing to park in his back yard.

Weary from her earlier walk and with her laborious efforts now, she continued doggedly on, mauling her lower lip in an effort to stop it trembling. But trembling she was when she reached the cottage, fumbling with the catch and steeling herself to take on the chin his mocking laughter as she entered.

He was not there. The place seemed empty, and she collapsed on to the settee, white-faced and low-spirited, angry both with herself and with him for doing what she had asked.

Lying back, she closed her eyes, only to open them again, having sensed a presence. The trembling hadn't completely receded.

'OK, so crow if you want to,' she challenged. 'I'm tired, I'm exhausted. I'm a fool to have left the car.' Her eyes came to blazing life. 'I don't care, do you hear? I don't care about anything...'

'Not even about Jerome?'

Was that what he thought was upsetting her? That she was still in love with his errant brother?

'Certainly not about *him*!' Which, no doubt in Leo Dower's mind, implied that if it wasn't her unrequited love of Jerome that was the cause it was the 'trouble' that he had supposedly brought on her.

She leaned back, eyes closed, feeling composure return. Yet a battle still raged within her—of wanting to fight this man, yet longing for comfort from those powerful arms. *And not just his arms*.

Her eyes flew open to rest on his mouth, his swept-back black hair, the darkly defined eyebrows, and those eyes, those unsettling, all-seeing eyes, that held secrets she, Rhea Hirst, would never hear...

To her horror, tears sprang, but she dashed them away, wishing her limbs would stop shaking, not just from shock now, but from some deep-down inner knowledge, so new, so frightening that she told herself it must never be allowed to erupt to the surface of her mind.

He was handing her a drink, his face expressionless. The alcohol was potent, but she finished it and handed him the glass as, slowly, calmness returned.

'I'm fine, thank you. You can call off the surveillance of my physical state.'

Even to her own ears it sounded ungrateful, but, she repeated to herself this time, she didn't care, she just didn't care. Did she?

The telephone rang in the living-room one evening as Rhea watched television. Alone, she wondered if she had time to fit the crutches into place and answer it before the caller gave up.

As she hauled herself upright and adjusted the crutches, Leo materialised from nowhere, taking the call. There was a room in the cottage which he kept locked but in which, while at home, he spent a lot of his time. In the few glimpses inside which Rhea had been allowed to snatch, it seemed to be fitted out as an office.

'Leo Dower.' Rhea thought she must have imagined the sharp intake of breath until he clipped, 'Jerome? Where the hell are you? You land me with yet another of your peccadilloes, then make a break for it. It's time you acknowledged your responsibilities and came back into circulation. So come on, brother, give.'

Leo beckoned to Rhea, who made it across to stand beside him.

'I don't want to talk to Jerome,' she whispered hoarsely. 'We've got nothing to say to each other.'

'Just listen,' said Leo, operating a switch on the telephone, at which Jerome's amplified voice came over loud and clear.

'I take it from your statement,' he said, speaking slowly, 'that you had a visit from—er—a lady called Rhea, Rhea Hirst?'

'I did. She's still here.'

'Oh, dear,' with false sympathy. 'You mean you haven't been able to pay her off like you have the others? Now I wonder why?'

His tone implied that he knew the answer.

'You'd agree with my description, would you?' he went on. 'A lady. She's made an impression on you, has she, so you haven't had the heart yet to tell her to go? You'd better cut her loose, brother, pronto. She's bad news.'

There seemed to be the faintest note of urgency in his voice, which his brother appeared to pick up, raising an eyebrow.

'She injured her foot—her ankle,' Leo said. 'She's in plaster, partly disabled. Get it, Jerome? She's here until she's able to walk unaided again. And I've a mind to keep her here until you come and get her, then do your duty by marrying her.'

There was a minor explosion at the other end. '*Marry her*? You must be joking! What do you take me for?'

'Yes, marry her and accept the responsibilities that paternity and fatherhood bestow on a begetter of children.'

Jerome gave a prolonged, choking cough. 'A *w-what*?' he stammered, recovering. 'She told you *that*?' He swore, making Rhea flinch. 'For Pete's sake, I only told her to get some money out of you to pay for the car I—er—bought from her.'

'He *stole* it,' Rhea intervened under her breath, but no one listened.

'So she's used the oldest trick in the book, has she, the cunning little bi——' Jerome checked, then amended '—beggar, to get me to tie the knot.' A pause, then a different, more persuasive tone. 'If you're so keen, Leo, to give the new generation of Dowers the benefit of a father and his—or her, as the case may be—rightful name, why don't you marry her yourself?'

Rhea expelled a furious breath and swung a crutch to move away. Leo's hand came out, grasping her arm, holding it.

'Ask her, Leo, see what she says. You never know your luck, pal.' There was barely suppressed laughter in Jerome's unrepentant voice. 'She's so hard up—did you know that?—she might say yes for the money—your money—in the bank. No doubt she's guessed by now what a wealthy guy you are. Oh, and tell her I'll pack up her things I found in the car and send them on. Bits and pieces of jewellery—junk, of course——'

'They were my mother's!' Rhea hissed furiously.

'And her squares and rectangles of weaving—tap-estries was the grand name she gave them—plus some-thing she called "batik". Has she told you, Leo, what an accomplished little *lady* she is? Must ring off—this call's costing me a fortune. Say "hi" to my darling ex-fiancée, will you?'

'Where are you, Jerome?' Leo rapped out.

'Ah, that's a secret. You won't find me walking into the noose that's waiting to strangle me.'

'What noose?'

'Why,' a long-drawn out laugh, 'marriage, of course, and the *fatherhood* you talked about. What else?' There was a click, then silence.

Rhea stifled a gasp. Jerome had played along with his brother's assumption that she was expecting a child, which meant that the idea was now fixed, hard as cement, in Leo's mind! Released at last from Leo's hold, she swung herself back to the settee.

Leo proceeded to walk up and down, hands pocketed, pausing at the windows which, at each end of the room, overlooked the rear and front gardens. He seemed to be fighting a battle, or was it anger? But if anyone has a right to be angry, Rhea thought, I have. It was she who had suffered at Jerome's hands, not Leo.

'Even now you won't condemn him, will you?' Rhea thrust thickly into the silence. 'I'm the one you've branded as no good. I'm just passing through your life, so I don't signify, do I? You're no doubt arguing inside your head that blood's thicker than water. Brother means more than brother's cast-off woman, so you accept his word against hers. Well,' her own head lifted proudly, 'I can take it, all the blame, all the censure. I've taken so much in the past few months; a little more, for a little longer, won't break my spirit.'

He came to stand beside her, and she felt the full impact of him, his power, his magnetism. His very posture seemed to threaten, his legs slightly apart, his strong thighs, his wide hips, lean waist above the waistband. So much masculinity had her senses swimming, but she refused to raise her head and meet his eyes. All the same, she had to. His hand came out and tilted her face, fastening around it so that she had to look him in the eye.

'So there's an idea.' The cynicism mouthed by his twisted lips clashed with the strange bleakness in his hard, handsome face. 'Since my dear brother Jerome refuses to do his duty, will you take me as your husband, Rhea Hirst?'

CHAPTER FIVE

HIDING her moist, bunched fists, Rhea did not, could not, answer. Speech had deserted her, her thoughts becoming scrambled like a secret message.

Her hatred of Jerome became paramount, pushing reason into second place. And since, by all accounts, this man in front of her made it his business constantly to connive with his brother, pacifying and paying off the women the brother had wronged, that hatred spilled over to encompass Leo Dower too.

His consideration in putting himself out to obtain medical attention for her—yes, of course, she was grateful for that, not to mention his offer of a roof until she had recovered from her disability. But such gestures arose only from his sense of duty, from his feeling of obligation to her because of her supposed treatment at his brother's hands. And this proposal of marriage arose from these sentiments too.

'There's no need, Mr Dower,' she said at last, 'to let your conscience drive you to take such a step as to offer marriage to someone you despise, as I know you despise me.'

He looked at her sharply, but, to her curiously intense disappointment, he did not deny her statement. He walked by.

'No doubt,' came from him bitingly, 'in your eyes Leo Dower would be a poor substitute for the man you really want.' He shrugged, walked away, came back. 'Get this, Rhea. No Dower is going to be born outside marriage if I have anything to do with it.'

'You—you mean you're so determined to give the—the new Dower you're so convinced is on its way a name that you'd even be willing to sacrifice your freedom?'

Those broad shoulders lifted and fell. '"My freedom"?' He returned to stand in front of her. 'What a curious expression! In these times, freedom, like a marriage, comes and goes.'

'All right, then, for the sake of your family name, you'd actually *tie* yourself to a woman you don't love and whom you look on with contempt, and always will?'

He stared unreadably into her eyes.

'So,' as if she had not spoken, as if she had actually agreed, 'you will marry me. Then, when the child is born and is registered as a Dower, you'll be free to do as you wish. Go or stay. A divorce would be one way of dealing with the situation. Separation, any other variation,' his shoulder lifted, 'it doesn't matter to me.'

So, Rhea thought, her mind still reeling under the impact of his suggestion—or had it really been an order?—Jerome had been right in one thing, even if he had been wrong in all the others. Leo did take life as it came... and went. Putting any woman out of his mind and moving on to the next and the next...

'I'd give you an allowance,' he was saying, 'sufficient to cover your needs and that of Jerome's——'

'There isn't going to be a child,' the declaration burst through her unguarded lips, 'so will you stop——?'

'You will not take that step,' he rasped, eyes dark as night, 'do you hear? You came to me for help because my brother refused to accept his responsibilities. I am therefore taking full responsibility for you on his behalf.' He walked away.

So he had misunderstood her outburst! Well, her conscience was clear, she had told him the truth and he had chosen to disbelieve it. He returned, his eyes holding hers. Unable to stand his penetrating gaze, Rhea looked elsewhere, but that look still burned through, so she covered her face to shut it out.

A hand touching her hair made her shiver. That hand slid slowly down her cheek, leaving a tingling trail. The pulses in her neck leapt as his fingers crept over her throat. The effect of his touch was so electric that it frightened her.

Hands fastened under her armpits and drew her to her feet. Still she refused to open her eyes. If only her breathing would even out, filling her lungs instead of manifesting itself in short jerks, shaking her.

Arms with the power to forge hard metal into flowing shapes pulled her to him. Lips, firm and cool and totally masculine, claimed hers, and she found her errant self responding, allowing her mouth to be caught and tantalised and played with, then completely possessed. Her arms began to let her down, lifting and clinging as her body swung this way and that as the fancy took the arms which held her.

'That,' he said thickly, as her eyes sprang wide and dismayed at the way her inner sexuality had responded to—worse, actually *collaborated* with—his, 'is all I wanted to know.'

He walked away again, leaving her strangely cold and inwardly trembling, her leg, the one that had supported her, so weak that she feared she would fall if she didn't find her seat again.

'I'd respect the fact that you're expecting Jerome's child,' he said coolly, as if the kiss had never happened, 'which means that it would be a marriage in name only. I'd ask nothing of you, no sacrificial acts of intimacy, or so-called love. You would simply wear my ring until your life after the event settled down and you found yourself able to cope with your changed circumstances. Then I'd release you. No recriminations, no conditions to be fulfilled. At a time convenient to us both, the marriage would end.'

There won't be an 'event'! The words shrieked inside her head. But hadn't she tried just now to tell him the truth, and hadn't he misinterpreted? So her lips stayed sealed on her secret.

'You wouldn't want for anything,' he was saying.

'Not even—even after the divorce?' she broke in with a bitterness that surprised her.

'Not even after that. Nor for the rest of your life.'

Divorce? Her inner self was actually contemplating accepting his proposal? Why not? a voice whispered. Then it came to her like thunder from a clear blue sky— what better way, she thought recklessly, to wreak that revenge she longed to have on the Dower family...a kind of payment to her by them for all the misery and unhappiness that its younger son had brought crashing down on to her head?

She released the breath she didn't even realise she was holding.

'Yes,' she answered, eyes bright, head held high, 'I'll marry you. For all the reasons you said.'

Two days after the cast was removed from Rhea's leg, the wedding took place. During the ceremony the best man, Vince Adley, an old friend of Leo's, took care of the walking stick which Rhea still needed.

Nathan was there, acting as one of the witnesses, Leo's uncle Timmy being the other. To Rhea's immense relief, there was no sign of Sonya.

Rhea's cream-shaded dress was fashioned to follow her shape, and if Leo, in his swiftly appraising glance as she had walked slowly down the stairs, had wondered at her persisting slimness, he had made no comment. Her satin shoes matched the dress, likewise the cream satin ribbon around the navy wide-brimmed hat which framed her face.

Where the wedding breakfast was concerned, had she been a true bride, both loving and loved, she could not have asked for more. At a fashionable hotel in the town, among flowers and bridal decorations, they were served with choice dishes and wines. Champagne, the best, flowed, and, to Rhea's astonishment, Leo had even taken the trouble to order a wedding cake. A miniature loving couple, made of icing, stood amid swirls of sugar flowers.

The handful of guests whom Leo had invited insisted that the bride and groom stood together, knife poised, while cameras snapped and whirred. Rhea did her best to hide her embarrassment, part of her wanting to cry out, Don't bother, please. This is a phoney wedding, we don't love each other at all. But, to her dismay, the other part of her wanted it to be real, to be meaningful and truly loving, followed by a fulfilling, not an empty marriage.

Laughter and warm feelings filled the room, jokes, largely at Leo's expense, flying back and forth as the wedding breakfast progressed. Carrie, Vince Adley's sister, tall and curly-haired, kept smiling at Rhea as if for encouragement, making her acutely aware of her own tension and lack of spontaneity.

Seated beside her, their arms brushing now and then, Leo seemed to have noticed.

'By marrying me,' he whispered, his mouth close to her ear, 'you haven't signed your death warrant, merely taken my name for the sake of things to come. Nothing's permanent, and nothing's changed, except *your* name. Will you play out your role as the happy bride, with or without the blushes, for the next hour or two at least? If it's any help, you look beautiful.'

Rhea turned to him, secretly pleased by his compliment, although she knew it to be false. 'There's really no need to flatter me,' she responded tartly, then caught a look in his eyes that set her pulses leaping. Had he been sincere, after all? Her smile broke through like the sun from behind a blanket of cloud.

'That's better,' he murmured, turning her by the shoulders and placing his cool, wine-tinged lips on hers. From the men there was an ironic cheer, while the women happily applauded.

Now, seated beside a silent and strangely preoccupied Leo, Rhea leaned back tiredly, staring out at the passing scenery. It was the state of her emotions that troubled her most. Even now, just thinking about that careless kiss he had given her simply to please their audience, she found her heart beating faster, the touch and taste of his mouth on hers lingering alarmingly.

'You did well.' His abrupt praise broke into her reverie, startling her.

'You mean you've discovered an unexpected side of me?' she returned, still staring out. 'You're surprised to find that I can role-play? You asked me to, remember?'

He shrugged, accelerating to climb a hill. 'Whatever.' After a pause, 'You rose to the occasion.'

'Thank you,' she responded stiffly, then removed her hat, twisting to place it on the rear seat.

The rice had rained on them, confetti floated down, cries of 'Good luck!' following them. Plainly their guests had managed to fool themselves into believing it was a love match after all.

'My parents,' Rhea found herself explaining, 'loved having people around them, and they entertained a great deal. My mother suffered from indifferent health, so sometimes I took her place. All my education, my home environment, conditioned me into acting the sparkling hostess, no matter how I might feel.'

Eyes on the road, Leo remarked, 'You must tell me some time.'

'There's nothing to tell.' But there was, so much that it would fill volumes.

There would be no honeymoon. She had insisted on this from the start, and Leo had merely shrugged in his usual offhanded way. As they crossed the ancient bridge spanning the river, something deep inside her leapt at the sight of Leo's cottage.

In the few weeks that she had lived there, she was secretly forced to acknowledge that she had grown to love the place. Wasn't it ironic, she asked herself, as Leo parked in his usual place, that she had come to feel a deep affection for this man's home, if not for the man himself? Sensitivity to his presence, acute and disturbing though it was, she told herself firmly, must not be mistaken for anything but irritation.

The country silence came rushing in through the opened windows.

'Rhea?' Steel-grey eyes, resolute and inscrutable as they usually were, rested on her face. He reached out and removed something from the silky tendrils, holding it out. The gesture reminded her of the day they had first met, when he had extracted a piece of grass from her hair.

Now it was a piece of confetti, tiny, heart-shaped, which he placed in the palm of her hand, closing her fingers over it. She looked at it and put it in her purse. She never wanted to lose that minuscule heart; it was a symbol of something which she knew for certain would for ever be beyond her reach, but keep it she would.

Taking her other hand, Leo looked at the ring which a couple of hours earlier he had placed on her wedding finger.

'You may kiss the bride.' The traditional words drifted into her mind. And, in front of the wedding guests, he had done so, sweetly, softly... and totally without passion. All the same, her lips still felt that kiss as if it had only at that moment been placed there.

'Yes?' It seemed that it hadn't been a question since he shook his head. 'I——' She moistened her lips. 'Thank you for what you've done, but——'

Now, a voice shrieked inside her head, tell him the truth... tell him *this minute*. The revenge you planned to have on the Dower family—now you legally wear his ring... this is it, your moment of triumph, of glorious victory. 'But——' It wasn't necessary to marry me, because there's no new Dower on the way... The words stuck fast, almost choking her.

Leo swung open his door and came round to help her out. The moment had passed, the time for confession receding into the background. The relief was so strong that it frightened her. It didn't mean—did it?—that, for some reason she couldn't fathom, she was actually glad to have become this man's wife?

In the living-room he left her and went upstairs, coming down in T-shirt and jeans, his working clothes.

'If you need my help for any reason,' he said, gesturing to the telephone, 'you know where to find me.'

Rhea sank back in the chair, anticlimax swamping her. So this was it—marriage to Leo Dower, a house full of silence? The clamour—for what? conversation, companionship, *love*?—was all in her head. With the aid of her walking stick, she pulled herself up the stairs and slowly divested herself of her wedding outfit.

The hat she replaced carefully in its box, the dress and jacket she slid on to a hanger. Pulling off her shoes, she stared at them, at their shining, *virgin* newness. Drawing a shuddering breath, she drew back her arm and hurled them one by one through the open window.

Hours later she stirred to darkness, her face damp with the tears that had shaken her slender frame until an exhausted sleep had claimed her. Something had disturbed her and, opening her eyes, she saw Leo, frowning down at her. He held up the shoes, one in each hand. 'How come?' he asked with a hint of amusement. 'Did they jump out of their own accord? Maybe they fancied a riverside walk in the dark without their owner?'

She had to smile. 'I was letting off steam.'

'Some steam! Do you blow your top every time you get yourself married?'

'Every time,' another smile, less shaky this time, 'without exception.'

'Was I your imaginary target?'

'Yes,' she answered. And the circumstances, and...everything you don't know about. She became conscious of her partly undressed state, her silk slip having ridden high above her thighs.

Seeming to notice her embarrassment, Leo dropped the shoes and slid his hand beneath her thighs, easing the silky fabric down. Her mouth opened on a gasp, but she masked it with a strangled 'Don't!'

His touch was electric, stinging her violently like a shock from the mains. Never, she vowed, would she let him touch her again. Its effect was so devastating that she did not dare to imagine what it would do to her if she ever...he ever...

'For God's sake, I'm your husband!' He seemed angry, but so was she.

'In name only,' she hit back. 'You'd ask nothing, you promised. If—if you want me to regard you as a man of principle, as you seem to think you are, then keep that promise. It was the basis of this marriage contract we entered into.'

'Then why have you been crying?'

Why? How could she answer when she didn't even know herself? She sat up slowly, to give herself time. 'Because——'

'I'm not Jerome?'

'No, no!' But let him think that, she chided herself; it was as good a reason as any, wasn't it? 'My foot,' she added for good measure.

'It still hurts?'

She nodded, averting her eyes from his overpowering masculinity. Looking at him in the semi-darkness, she felt something begin to stir inside her, some deep, inexplicable feeling... Surely it wasn't a sense of *longing*? Of course it wasn't. Fatigue, more likely, reaction to the long day, and all that it had contained, meaningless though it had been.

'That,' she temporised. 'And—and other things.'

To her relief, yet perversely to her disappointment, he turned, his measured footsteps carrying him away.

He had breakfasted and gone by the time Rhea made her way downstairs. She wondered, on this first day of their marriage, whether he would bring his sandwiches and his uncle Timmy as he had on her first day there, but he did not.

''Morning, dear.' Mrs Litton, Leo's twice-weekly help, let herself in and smilingly surveyed her employer's new wife. 'Nice wedding, was it, love? I bet you looked fit to eat in that dress I saw hanging on the door of your wardrobe!' She inspected Rhea's face. 'Your foot still troubling you? You look a bit pale.'

Swiftly Rhea turned on a brilliant smile, doing her best to fit Mrs Litton's idea of a radiant bride. 'You're right about my foot, but otherwise I'm fine, thanks.'

The lady help, romantically satisfied, went about her business, getting through her work with extra speed. Did Mrs Dower mind? Mrs Litton asked, leaving a light lunch on a tray nearby. 'My daughter and her kiddies are coming for a couple of days.'

Mrs Dower, startled by being thus addressed, and wanting to declare that inside she was still Miss Hirst, said she didn't mind at all.

Late morning the postman delivered a heavy box, obligingly carrying it into the cottage. 'From foreign parts,' he commented, pointing to the stamps and the postmark.

'Foreign' to people living there, Rhea knew, could sometimes mean from another part of the country, but this time it had meant exactly that. The box had been

mailed in Singapore, and Rhea guessed at once who had
sent it.

Herewith your rubbish, but you won't get your car
back. It's mine now, safely locked away. Don't I deserve it after everything? Tell my brother not to jump
to the conclusion that if he drops everything and flies
over here he'll find me. I'm en route, and I'm not
telling where. Has he married you yet? I guess he has.
He's a stickler for doing the right thing. Unlike me,
I hear you say. Hope you enjoy the patter of tiny feet.
Ha! Happy memories, yes? Jerome.

At the last brash phrase, Rhea almost tore the note
into shreds, but restrained herself. Leo had a right to see
its contents. She was reaching into the box, surrounded
by the items she had already withdrawn, when there came
a knock and the turn of the door-handle.

'How's the newly-wed?' asked Nathan, looking with
interest at the articles scattered over the floor.

Rhea knew that for Nathan she didn't have to put on
the 'blushing bride' act. He, like Leo's other close
friends, knew the truth, or what they assumed was the
truth.

'Happy now I've got my things back,' she answered,
gesturing to the articles all around her. Her mother's
jewellery she had carried up to her room and locked
away.

Nathan did not ask 'back from whom?' 'Hey, what's
all this?' he exclaimed, kneeling beside Rhea and gazing
around as if he had found buried treasure. 'Whose
handiwork is this? And this?' He picked up pieces of
unfinished embroidery, squares of hessian and linen,
rough sketches on graph paper, triangles of canvas,
lengths of material both plain and dyed.

'Mine,' Rhea told him with a smile. 'Just experiments
with designs and colours.'

'A hobby, you said. Craftsman that I am, looking at these I'm not fooled, Rhea. You're a professional.' He spoke almost accusingly, and Rhea laughed.

'Maybe, maybe not. I'm qualified enough to make a living at this kind of work. Even to teach it if I want.'

'You're a dark horse, Rhea. Why?'

She shrugged and shook her head. Nathan knew her well enough not to probe. The door opened yet again, and Rhea's heart nearly leapt sideways as Leo strolled in. Eyes narrowing a fraction, he glanced from one to the other, then at the contents of the box.

Rhea thought he deserved an explanation. 'Jerome sent them back to me. He kept his word.'

'You sound surprised.'

'I have reason to be,' she murmured, picking up a square of fabric.

'No car? Or rather, promise of its return?'

She shook her head, handing him Jerome's note. After scanning it, he threw it aside. 'I get the feeling it's coded.'

Rhea looked up quickly, but he said nothing. This man was, for her peace of mind, too quick on the uptake.

Nathan rose, pointing. 'That girl has been pulling the wool over our eyes.' Rhea's heart leapt again. Had Nathan guessed her secret? It seemed he hadn't. 'All this—this work, it's all hers. Would you believe?'

'OK, Rhea, enlighten us.' Leo's voice was low and compelling, and she found herself saying,

'I'd have told you, but it didn't somehow seem relevant. I've got a degree in art.' She looked directly at Leo.

'You have?' said Nathan, sounding strangled.

'So.' Leo this time. 'Why the mystery?'

Tingles ran down her spine and she wished she could read his expression. As his hand came out to help her up, she jerked in surprise. He did not release her hand, clasping it in a handshake. 'As one craftsman to another, Rhea Hirst, welcome to the club.'

Distantly she heard Nathan say, 'I echo that.'

Leo had called her 'Hirst', but it didn't matter. Her heart nearly danced for joy. For the first time ever, she glimpsed warmth in Leo's eyes, the merest flicker, but to her it was as warming as a fire on a cold day. He released her hand.

'Yes, well,' said Nathan, looking from Leo to her. Was he thinking that, in spite of everything, the man who now called himself her husband had some feeling for her after all?

How wrong he would be, Rhea thought.

'I just called in to say "hi",' Nathan added. 'I'm on my way to the town.' He smiled broadly at Rhea. 'Wait until I tell the group about the accomplished lady we now have in our midst! They'll welcome you with open arms. You—er—' with a quick glance at Leo and making for the door '—you won't let them down, will you? What I mean is, you'll agree to meet them?'

'Of course. I'll be delighted to meet them all.' With a defiant lift of the head, 'With or without Leo's permission.'

'What was that supposed to mean?' asked Leo when Nathan had gone, picking up Jerome's note again.

Rhea's shoulders lifted. 'Nathan seemed to think that now we've gone through a marriage ceremony we operate as a single unit. That we can't bear to be apart, that we tell each other our movements and——'

Leo, reading the note, did not seem to be listening. '"Happy memories,"' he quoted. 'Which means that, whatever you may say about your association with my brother——'

'He was being facetious. There may have been happy times, but my memories of him now and everything to do with him are the very opposite of happy.'

'You really do bear him a grudge for what he did to you, don't you?'

'Who wouldn't?' she retorted. 'He changed the course of my life completely...' Then she realised what he had meant. So we're back to the 'baby' issue, she thought miserably. Some time soon she would have to tell him.

To her relief, Leo changed course.

'What was the make of your car? The one he "borrowed"?'

'One of the very few that might well keep its value while being locked away.'

'A Rolls? You owned a Rolls-Royce?'

'It was my father's, the only thing I managed to salvage from the mess.' Why did she feel she had to defend herself? 'I thought I told you. The entire business toppled. It was failing for some time before he, and my mother, died.'

For the rest of the day, Rhea worked on the items Jerome had returned to her. With Leo's iron and with loving care she pressed the specimens, then labelled them methodically.

Looking up from her work, she realised not only that she was hungry, but also that she was still alone. She made a light supper for herself and, having cleared away, stared out at the darkening moorland.

Pulling on a jacket over her T-shirt, and pushing her feet into walking shoes, she found her stick and went outside. She looked right, left, then right again. Something drew her that way, over the old stone bridge and down the road that led to the village. And the forge.

If he was not there, she would swallow her pride, remind herself that he was a free agent, despite the ceremony they had gone through, and force herself not to be jealous. After all, Sonya Selby had a great deal to offer a man. Why should he leave her arms to return to the woman he had married simply to protect the new member of the Dower family he was so convinced was on its way?

If Leo was there—well, she'd turn back, wouldn't she? Telling herself that at least she knew where he was. The telephone? That, he had said, she could use if she needed him. Which she didn't and, she told herself, never would.

He was there—the ringing strike of hammer on metal told her that in advance. So why were her feet still carrying her on... and into the semi-darkness?

His back was to her, but he paused, hammer raised, as if sensing, as he had the first time, that she was there. He turned, staring at her just as he had before.

Flickering and uncertain though the interior of the old forge was, the impact on her senses of his height, his muscled breadth, the sheen upon his torso, was even greater than that first time.

As if drawn by an invisible force, Rhea went towards him and stood leaning heavily on her stick. Why had she come? If he asked her, she wouldn't know. All she did know was that she had forcibly to hold herself back from going to him, touching his chest, moving his arm until it encircled her, putting her lips against his...

Slowly his hand released the hammer, its clatter making her shiver—or was it the look in his eyes? He did not, on this occasion, pull on his T-shirt out of courtesy and politeness.

'You want me?' His tone was clipped, discouraging.

She came to her senses. Of course he did not want her here! 'No. Thank you.' She turned to go.

'Liar.' He moved to cut off her retreat. 'You *want* me. And you want this.'

His arms swung her round, her stick hitting the ground. There was no mercy in the way he roped her body to his, no consideration in the way his mouth descended. There was a world of sensuality in the way his lips crushed hers, his tongue rasping against their tender skin until she submitted and allowed him thrusting access. Without restraint he plundered the secret moistness of her mouth, disregarding her throaty cries, only relenting and softening when her resistance died away and she melted into him.

His head lifted, although his lips remained in tingling contact with hers. 'You wanted that,' he said thickly. 'You wanted a little *romance*, did you, to sweeten your memory of that sham marriage ceremony we shared yesterday?'

'No, I——' She shook her head, only to hear him laugh deep in his throat.

'Don't lie again, lady. I gave you what you came for. Or——' he drawled, drawing away enough to look down at her warm, upturned face '—am I to regard that as just a preliminary to——'

'No! You'd be breaking our agreement, breaking your word.' If he made love to her now, he would guess—what would he guess? What she hadn't allowed even herself to guess, nor even to think about. 'You can keep your lovemaking!' she heard herself cry. She struggled to free herself and he let her go, his expression sardonic. 'For your beautiful girlfriend,' she added, retrieving her stick. 'You think I'm not intelligent enough to have guessed?'

His broad shoulders shrugged off her questions. 'Oh, you're intelligent,' he said sarcastically. 'I've never doubted that.' He turned to replenish the fire.

Rhea found her eyes upon his back, closing them fiercely until she had managed to discipline the feelings the mere sight of his moving unclothed torso aroused.

Desperate to bring the emotional temperature down to normal levels, she moved around the uneven stone floor. Sensitive to the atmosphere of the place, she could almost swear she could hear the whinnying of horses of olden times.

With a professional eye, she studied the metallic shapes that were scattered about the place.

It was the artist in her that asked, 'Are these designs experimental, or part of a whole?'

'Both.' Leo moved to stand beside her, and only with the greatest difficulty did she keep her reactions to him on an intellectual plane.

'I didn't realise there was a place for a forge in modern life.'

'A fair comment, coming from a suburbanite, as you are.' No criticism there, just a simple observation. 'But you're not alone in thinking that by a long way. My uncle Timmy has enough work to keep him going for a long time to come.'

'Which is why you break away from your business responsibilities now and then to help him?'

'Who's been talking? Nathan? Yes, I guessed. I don't just come here to help my uncle. To me, it's a relaxation as well as a hobby. Timmy says it's an obsession with me.' His broad shoulders lifted. 'Whatever, he's glad of my help.' After a moment he added, 'It's the constant challenge, having to fulfil tricky orders, that I can't resist. Not to mention,' with a quizzical lift of the eyebrow, 'as you will no doubt appreciate and understand, the demand on one's creativity, that keeps me tied to it.'

'I understand,' she replied fervently. 'I feel that constant drive myself.'

'I guessed that.'

Rhea revelled in the way he was confiding in her, talking to her as an equal. 'What kind of things do you make?' she asked.

'We repair the kind of objects that people treasure, like much-loved spades, gardening forks; things people value, like old kettles. Obvious items like horseshoes, forged door hinges, window catches for renovation jobs. Once Timmy and I rehabilitated a wind-battered cockerel from an ancient church tower.'

'And creative work? Like those gates I heard you talking about to Miss Selby?'

'Decorative folding iron gates. Larger contracts like that, yes. They're what interest me most.' Leo wandered back to his work. 'It's a traditional coke-fired forge,' he explained. 'Timmy and I decided against changing to a more up-to-date gas-fired model.'

He turned towards the flames, their scarlet heat dancing over his tough arms. Rhea watched him at the anvil, and winced as he handled with nonchalant assurance pieces of red-hot metal he had drawn from the fire. Sparks flew and she held her breath as the incandescent rod kept inching ever closer to his horrifyingly vulnerable skin. Why she should worry in case he got hurt, she didn't know, but worry she did.

She sat on a battered wooden upright chair, her walking stick leaning against her side. Her ears rang with the sound his hammer strikes were making, reverberating around the wide, low-ceilinged building and ricocheting against the stone walls.

His face drew her eyes, the intense concentration in all its angles illumined by the glow of the white-hot metal he was manipulating. His full lips, which only a few minutes ago had been crushed against hers, were compressed by the determination with which he handled and controlled the object he hammered into submission. He leaned forward, the better to produce the shape he required, his wide shoulders curving slightly, his flesh gleaming.

Rhea was certain he had forgotten her presence, but some minutes later, apparently satisfied with the form he had created, he put down his tools and looked up, as if he had been perfectly aware of her the whole time. Taking a towel from a pile, he rubbed at his moisture-laden neck and shoulders, drying his arms and lifting them, revealing the patches of hair, moving the towel downwards to skim over the curling mat on his chest. Discarding the towel, he looked at her, and the words he spoke were to turn her whole world upside down.

'Tell me something.' He moved to stand in front of her, arms folded, his physique daunting, although a flicker of a smile brought a momentary softening to his expression. 'I guess I should have asked before, but typically man-like, as a woman would no doubt say, it slipped my mind. When is Jerome's child due to be born?'

CHAPTER SIX

RHEA'S heart began to pound, her breaths wrenched from her lungs. This, she told herself emphatically, was the moment she had been longing for. This was the moment when she wreaked her revenge on the Dower family, the revenge she had sworn to have from the time Jerome's treachery and fraudulent behaviour had been revealed to her.

It had been a reckless revenge that she had embarked upon, she saw that now. How *could* she have chosen such a way of achieving her ends? But didn't she deserve some reparation for the havoc and pain Jerome had caused in her life? The way he had contributed to her father's financial downfall? And, eventually, to her parents' deaths? If she had chosen this way of evening things up with the Dower family, could she really be blamed?

Leo stood there, towering over her, his expression unreadable in the shadowy semi-darkness, and she realised what a terrible error she had made. Like a lightning flash, her intuition revealed to her the real reason she had agreed to marry this man.

Beyond a shadow of doubt, when she was about to be thrown out of his life for ever, she knew that she had fallen in love with Leo Dower the moment she had set eyes on him...and that she loved him more than she had ever loved another living being.

Her mouth had grown parched, her throat rough with tension. She answered, 'I'm not expecting Jerome's child.' As he didn't seem to comprehend, she added, slowly and clearly, 'There isn't going to be a baby.'

It was as though he had become carved in stone. A spark leapt from the fire. Even if it had started a blaze Rhea doubted if he would have stirred. Then slowly, gropingly, he picked up his T-shirt, with mechanical movements pulling it over his head. Eyes a steely grey, the look in them frightening in its intensity, he said, 'Are you telling me that you "lost" the child before you came here, then proceeded to pretend you were still carrying it?'

Rhea shook her head. When *would* he understand, accept the truth?

'Jerome didn't make me pregnant——'

His lips tautened into a snarl. 'But someone else did, then you pretended it was Jerome's?'

'No!' she almost shrieked. 'Don't you see? I've never expected a child. I——' It had to be said, and right now. She swallowed hard. She didn't love this man, she hated him, didn't she? So why wasn't she enjoying her revenge, instead of standing there attempting to explain her actions? 'I married you,' she flung at him, 'to get even with the Dower family, because of all the terrible things Jerome did to me, to my life.'

'And you're trying to tell me those "terrible things" were completely unconnected with a pregnancy that my brother caused? Oh, no, that won't wash. I can't believe what you're saying. I've been on the receiving end of too many demands for payment for the expectation and birth of Jerome's unborn but oncoming offspring, careless as he is, and as the women have been that he's chosen to sleep with.'

'I've never expected Jerome's child. You have to believe me!'

He moved nearer, face twisted with anger. 'When I've seen it in writing in the note he sent you? Where he referred to the "patter of tiny feet" to come? To me, that can mean only one thing.'

He had taken Jerome's note seriously! 'He was joking, Leo. He knew the situation——'

'Did he?' His hands on her arms forced her to her feet. 'Did you tell him you'd had an abortion? Isn't *that* the true situation?'

'No, because, I keep telling you, it wasn't true!'

'Yet you came here, accepted my hospitality, would have accepted my money if I'd offered it to you as I offered it to all the others? Then gone on your way if you hadn't hurt yourself and been forced to stay here? Not to mention,' cuttingly, 'accepting my offer to marry you. A novel way, you no doubt thought, of not just taking the very generous hand-out I gave to the others—to you, cocooned by your father's wealth, a tiny amount, no doubt—but, as my wife, gaining limitless access to my bank account? Which meant,' with a sneer, 'that I'd be able to keep you in the comfort to which you'd grown accustomed.'

His fury, all the more powerful for being controlled, was at white heat, more dangerous even than the incandescent metal he drew from the fire. As he spoke, Rhea was sure that sparks flew, hitting her, searing her skin. How, she asked herself again, could she have been so foolish as to choose this man as her means of wreaking revenge?

'My God,' he was saying, 'at least those other women were honest. At least they admitted bluntly that they wanted—would be completely satisfied with—the lump sum Jerome had promised would come their way. Better educated as you were, you were far more cunning, weren't you?' His teeth snapped and he seized her shoulders, then contemptuously threw her from him. He walked a few paces. 'You rid yourself of Jerome's little burden, then came——'

'For the hundredth time, I didn't!' she cried. 'Let me tell you something. Your wonderful brother Jerome is a fraud, a thief, a——' 'Murderer' she almost said.

He swung round. 'Call him names, would you, names that could be actionable, simply because he broke the engagement and stole your car?'

She shook her head, realising how useless it was trying to break down in his mind the high wall he had erected around his brother's integrity. There seemed to be no way open to her of getting him to accept the truth.

Hadn't his uncle Timmy told her their family story, how protective Leo had been since childhood towards his younger brother? So how could she ever expect him to believe anything but good about Jerome?

'I'll pack and leave,' Rhea told him heavily.

'You will?' he rasped. 'You realise that would be admitting your guilt, tacitly agreeing that I'm right in accusing you of having had an abortion prior to coming here? And of accepting my proposal of marriage under false pretences?'

'Would that matter? I wouldn't be here to hear the gossip.' Rhea lifted her shoulders. How bitter her revenge tasted now! 'I just want to get on with my life. And—' she raised her eyes to his '—and allow you to get on with yours.'

Leo moved closer, holding her gaze. 'Exactly why,' he asked curiously, 'did you marry me?'

'Because I——' The truth so nearly burst from her! But even if she had told him she loved him he would have laughed in her face. 'I told you why.' There was a long silence. 'OK, you win,' she conceded falsely. 'I was after your money. And the usefulness to me of your position in life,' she threw in for good measure. 'Plus the benefit of the Dower name.' She had meant to sound cynical, but it came out levelly as if she had honestly meant it.

He nodded as if he had believed every word. How ironic, she thought, that he'd accepted her lies as the truth, yet when she had told him the truth he had regarded it as a lie.

'Where would you go?' he asked.

'On leaving here? Youth hostels, cheap hotels.'

'Not back to Jerome?'

'*Jerome*? Oh, no, thank you. I wouldn't know where to find him, would I?'

Too late she realised that he had probably taken her words to mean that if she had known of Jerome's whereabouts, she would have had no hesitation in joining him.

Hands deep in pockets, he regarded her for a long time. She grew uncomfortable under his scrutiny and stood up, reaching for her stick. His hand came out, taking it from her.

'I've come to a decision,' he declared, tight-lipped. 'You'll remain here as my wife—which you are—for as long as it takes for our marriage, shall we say, to be "given a chance"? Then, despite our "efforts", it can appear to be failing. Then I might—*might*—reconsider the position.'

'But a divorce,' Rhea cried protestingly. 'You promised—— '

'After the birth, I said. But, according to you, there won't be a birth, will there? Which absolves me from that promise.' He moved towards her, making her skin prickle, standing close enough for her to feel his breath on her lips. Part of her wanted to back away, but that recalcitrant other part wanted to close the tiny gap that separated them and...

'You've sold yourself, Rhea Hirst,' he said, his voice low, tone menacing, sending a *frisson* of fear through her nervous system, 'into my keeping. By marrying me, you don't know what a dangerous game you've embarked upon.' In the half-darkness and the ruby glow from the dying fire, he looked devilish and dark and handsome, with a hardness that caused an icy sensation to shiver all down her spine.

'It's—well, it's just a matter of sitting it out,' she said, affecting a careless shrug, 'long enough to convince your

NO RISK, NO OBLIGATION TO BUY...NOW OR EVER!

GUARANTEED

PLAY "ROLL A DOUBLE" AND GET AS MANY AS FIVE FREE GIFTS!

HERE'S HOW TO PLAY:

1. Peel off label from front cover. Place it in space provided at right. With a coin, carefully scratch off the silver dice. This makes you eligible to receive two or more free books, and possibly another gift, depending on what is revealed beneath the scratch-off area.

2. Send back this card and you'll receive brand-new Harlequin Presents® novels. These books have a cover price of $2.99 each, but they are yours to keep absolutely free.

3. There's no catch. You're under no obligation to buy anything. We charge nothing – ZERO – for your first shipment. And you don't have to make any minimum number of purchases – not even one!

4. The fact is thousands of readers enjoy receiving books by mail from the Harlequin Reader Service® months before they're available in stores. They like the convenience of home delivery and they love our discount prices!

5. We hope that after receiving your free books you'll want to remain a subscriber. But the choice is yours – to continue or cancel, anytime at all! So why not take us up on our invitation, with no risk of any kind. You'll be glad you did!

NOT ACTUAL SIZE

You'll look like a million dollars when you wear this lovely necklace! Its cobra-link chain is a generous 18" long, and the multi-faceted Austrian crystal sparkles like a diamond!

"ROLL A DOUBLE!"

PLACE LABEL HERE

SCRATCH HERE

SEE CLAIM CHART BELOW

106 CIH AKW6
(U-H-P-08/93)

YES! I have placed my label from the front cover into the space provided above and scratched off the silver dice. Please rush me the free books and gift that I am entitled to. I understand that I am under no obligation to purchase any books, as explained on the back and on the opposite page.

NAME _____

ADDRESS _____ APT. _____

CITY _____ STATE _____ ZIP CODE _____

CLAIM CHART

	4 FREE BOOKS PLUS FREE CRYSTAL PENDANT NECKLACE	
	3 FREE BOOKS	
	2 FREE BOOKS	

CLAIM NO.37-829

friends and neighbours that we're not compatible. You've just said as much. Then I'll pack my things and get out of your life.'

'In *my* time, my dear wife,' the endearment was charged with sarcasm, scraping her nerves, 'in my own time. Not yours.'

He pressed against her and she thought his arms were coming round her, but it was his eyes that stroked her lips, not his mouth, and she forced herself to quell the treacherous uprush of disappointment.

'You've got to let me go,' she heard herself protesting. 'You take life, and women, with equal ease. Jerome told me so, and, from my comparatively small knowledge of you, I've seen that he was right. So why is it so important that you feel you have to convince your acquaintances that you're putting yet another woman out of your life?'

'You believed Jerome, those stories he told you about me? You didn't for one minute think they might simply be brotherly comments?'

They just had to be true! Yet, as she had discovered, Jerome *had* lied to her many times. Any thought that the 'stories' might not be true filled her with dread, a sense of being captured, imprisoned, and that he might never let her go.

'You mean—the women in your life,' she asked, 'they've never come and gone?' Leo stared down at her, still disturbingly close. Since he didn't answer, Rhea assumed that that side of his personal history was, as far as she was concerned, a closed book. 'All the same, you made a promise about this marriage of ours and——' she suddenly remembered '—as Jerome said in his note, you're a stickler for doing the right thing——'

'It all depends, doesn't it, what that "right thing" might be?'

Unnoticed, his arms had crept round her, holding her loosely. Now they were tightening and his head was lowering slowly, his eyes on her lips, his hand pressing against the back of her head, arm hooked around her slender waist. 'And this,' he murmured, his eyelids drooping, 'is the "right thing" at this moment. Don't you agree?'

Rhea felt the late-evening stubble abrasive against her skin, his wide mouth playing with hers, persuasive and persistent, parting her lips, his tongue invading and withdrawing until her inner mouth almost hungered for the taste of him. Yet she didn't want him kissing her, didn't want her body to succumb as it was doing, loving the touch of his hand on her breast...*how* had it got there?

The telephone broke through her gasp at his stroking fingers' audacity, demanding attention. Eyes pin-points in the fireglow—it was dark outside now—he uttered a curse and turned to silence it, her cotton top sliding down into place as he withdrew his hand.

'Yes?' shot curtly into the phone. 'Hi, Timmy,' barely tolerant, but polite. 'You want something?'

Timmy's voice came over loud and clear in the stillness. 'You still there at the forge, Leo? You OK? I saw the light from the fire from my window and wondered if you'd left and forgotten to put it out.'

'I'm here, Timmy,' long-sufferingly. 'I'm OK.'

'Isn't it time, lad, you...?' A thoughtful pause. 'You alone? Or is Sonya——?'

'My *wife*, Timmy, my *wife* is with me.'

'Ah.' Silence, then, 'Isn't it time she was home and resting? What with her foot still not back to normal and the babby on its way?'

Through teeth that were gritted, his nephew offered, 'There's no baby expected, Timmy, there never was.'

'No—no babby? You can't mean it?' The disappointment in his voice cut Rhea to the heart.

'No child on its way. Rhea's come clean. She's told me the truth at last. All this time she's been lying to me——'

Rhea's hand shot out, taking Leo by surprise and seizing the phone. 'I've never lied, Uncle Timmy,' she cried, 'I tried telling Leo that I wasn't pregnant, but he—he wouldn't believe it.'

'You mean—you don't mean, dear, you—well, *lost* it before you came here?'

'That's what Leo kept thinking I meant. Uncle Timmy,' she declared, 'I only ever came here because Jerome had told me his brother would help me financially, until I found my feet again after... after...' But Timmy wouldn't believe what Jerome had really done, any more than Leo would. To them both, Jerome was the tops, a 'good lad', who could never do wrong.

'That Jerome,' he sighed, 'that other rascal of a nephew of mine,' at Timmy's tone, and listening to Timmy's choice of words Rhea knew she had been right in guessing that Dower would defend Dower, no matter what, 'he's bad to women, that he is.' No censure there, just a touch of indulgent amusement. 'He treats 'em like he gets chewing gum from a slot machine, then throws 'em away. And he had to do it to you, dear.' Rhea could almost see him shaking his head. 'After getting engaged to you, too. Are you *sure*, lass, there's no——'

Leo turned the tables and seized the phone from Rhea's unsuspecting hand. 'You have to accept it, Timmy. She's not pregnant.'

Timmy hadn't finished. 'What about your marriage, Leo? It's hardly begun. Even if your reason for marrying the lass doesn't exist now, you'll surely give your marriage a chance? You aren't going to send her away, are you?'

'Can you think of any good reason why not?' Leo half turned to eye her, apparently amused by her heightened colour, her indignation.

'She's a good lass, Leo, that's why,' came Timmy's unhesitating answer, 'whatever she might or might not have done. She's what you need. Better for you by far than that Sonya. You'll be a fool if you let her go.'

'I'll bear your advice in mind, Timmy,' Leo drawled. 'Thanks for ringing and checking up. Everything here's OK.' Cutting the call, but still speaking into the unreceptive mouthpiece, he added, 'When a woman tells me she's married me merely to use me as a weapon of revenge, she gets everything that's coming to her.' Slowly he replaced the receiver and leaned back, fingers pushed into his waistband, and fixed her with a steely gaze. 'Got that, Miss Hirst?'

'Who's breaking the moral rules now?' Rhea hit back, infuriated by his arrogance, but most of all worried by the implication behind his words. 'You promised you'd ask nothing of me. Now you're as good as threatening to break that promise.'

'That promise was made before you told me the truth. Of course I wouldn't have touched you if you really had been expecting Jerome's child, either before or after. Now you tell me it's not so?' He seemed yet again to be wanting confirmation.

'I repeat, it's not so. I'm not pregnant, never have been.'

His broad shoulders lifted and fell. 'OK.' A long pause, as if he were weighing up the pros and cons. 'So, as my lawful wedded wife, and in view of the outrageous reason you've given for taking up that role, as I said, you take the consequences. No holds barred. Any normal man needs a woman now and then. One day,' his mocking glance raked her slender figure, 'I might want you.' His tone implied 'if I could ever bring myself to touch you'. 'And if I do——' Another shrug. 'You'll be there to gratify my needs,' was, Rhea knew, his unspoken innuendo.

How could she ever have thought she loved this man? A flare of hatred came burning through the emotion she had told herself was love. It had, she argued, been the only way she had been able to face being married to him—fooling herself into believing she loved him.

She saw him once again as a Dower, one of whom had already wrecked her life as she had known it. She refused to allow this Dower to repeat the devastating exercise.

'You,' she exploded, fear mixing with a frightening wanton excitement, 'you're as unscrupulous as your precious brother! The Dower family,' she stepped forward and clicked her fingers in his face, 'I don't give that for them. No one, not even a *Dower* takes me against my will. Not even the man who, for a short time only, calls himself my husband!'

Lips drawn into a thin line, Leo reached out and caught her wrists, jerking them to her sides and pulling her body against his. She gave a choking cry. In stepping forward to balance herself, she had inadvertently used her injured foot.

He seemed to think that it was because his grip around her wrists was inflicting pain, but he did not give an inch, forcing her head back with the pressure of his mouth. Again she took into her the intoxicating taste of him as his merciless kiss ground into her lips, leaving them throbbing and quivering with tension. She sagged against him, her head on his shoulder, finding a fleeting sanctuary in the strength and hard comfort of him.

When he saw in the flickering half-light how white she was, he jeered, 'What's wrong? Don't my kisses please you? Don't they measure up to Jerome's?'

'My foot,' she managed, biting her lip with pain and sinking weakly down on to the stone-flagged floor, her arms extended as her wrists remained in his hold.

Cursing, he lifted her, gathering her into his arms. She tried to tell her head to stay upright, tried to scold it when it rooted once again for the shoulder it seemed to have developed a sudden liking for, resting there with a perverse contentment all the way outside. This man was her enemy, she lectured the suppliant self over whom she strangely seemed to have no power.

He lowered her with an aloof kind of care on to the rear seat and drove her home.

In her room, he looked down at her as she sat on the bed. 'Will you be able to manage, or do you want my help?' he asked distantly.

Angry with herself for allowing her body to be fooled by his momentary softening towards her, Rhea stared up. 'I wouldn't accept your help if it came with a fortune,' she declared belligerently.

But she just had, hadn't she? she reminded herself as he strode from the room. She had been accepting his help from the day she had arrived on his doorstep. And, she was forced to acknowledge, she would go on needing that help for some time to come.

Nathan discovered her ten days later seated on a fallen tree-trunk near the river bank. With her left hand she held a drawing-board firmly on her lap, while with her right she sketched the river scene.

'Hi,' he said. 'I was passing and thought I'd call in. Mind if I join you? Just carry on.' He sat beside her. 'I'll do my best not to disturb the artistic equilibrium.'

'Be my guest,' she answered with a smile. 'I'm only too glad to have company.'

He frowned. 'Feeling lonely? What about your husband? He's around, at the forge every day.'

He's not my husband, she wanted to say. Instead she answered with a shrug, 'Yes, he's around.' Let Nathan make what he likes of that, she thought.

Leo had indeed been around. He had filled the cottage, been within her hearing, her sight, near enough to touch if she had stretched out her hand. But scarcely a word had passed between them. Yes, she was feeling lonely, she could have confided to Nathan.

At night, she and Leo had gone their separate ways with a polite 'goodnight'. Rhea usually went up first, using the bathroom quickly to avoid meeting him there. He came up much later, and she had found herself listening to his footsteps, trying to work out his movements, wondering whether this—this was the night when he... But he hadn't. The door of his room had always closed firmly behind him. It was as though they were mere acquaintances, and she had to acknowledge that it was wearing her down, almost to screaming pitch.

She couldn't hide it from herself any more: that she would almost have welcomed that demand on her as his wife which, that evening in the forge, he had hinted that he might make one day. Anything, she thought, to release this pressure that was building inside her, tormenting her; anything—a quarrel, even—to be able to put into words the mounting feeling of resentment, of anger, of—yes, she had to accept, even of frustration. Let him get it over with, she had found herself thinking. I could grit my teeth and allow him nearer to me than I ever allowed Jerome, than I've ever allowed any man...

'That's good,' commented Nathan, looking over her shoulder. 'That's great. Is it a sketch in itself, or——?'

'A design for a batik wall-hanging. The bridge fascinates me—its shape, its brickwork, its enduring strength despite its age.'

'You're filling the scene with birds and plants that I can't see anywhere around. Artistic licence?'

Rhea laughed. 'I'm adding interest and colour. And movement.' She stopped work and looked around. 'What I don't feel it's possible to capture in a picture like this, and I'm not even going to try, is the naturally subdued light of the countryside, the flowing tranquillity.'

'The peace and quiet,' Nathan offered, 'that soothes mixed-up emotions?'

She looked at him curiously. 'You understand?'

He nodded. 'Only too well. I guess,' he took a long breath, 'tell me if I'm wrong or intruding, that you're finding a certain relationship as difficult to cope with as I found my—certain relationship.'

He was, she realised, talking about his separation from his wife. 'You're not wrong, Nathan. Or intruding.'

There was a long, comfortable silence. Rhea resumed her work, adding, erasing, shading in.

'When——' He hesitated, taking a breath, starting again, 'When the—er—event happens, what will you do?'

Rhea did not hesitate to enlighten him. 'There won't be an "event", Nathan.' He made a startled movement. 'It was never a possibility. A misunderstanding—crossed wires. You know?'

'Ah,' as if he understood, although her softly spoken statement hadn't explained a thing. 'Tonight,' he said at last, 'there's an informal meeting of members of the local craft club—coffee and biscuits. We'd be delighted, Rhea, if you'd come along. We usually take whatever small piece we're currently working on, keep ourselves occupied. Vince Adley's place. I'll call for you. Unless you've got other plans?'

Such as going places with my husband, he meant, Rhea filled in. She shook her head. 'Leo spends every evening at the forge—or so he says.'

He got the implication. 'Sonya—she's a bitch.'

Rhea's heart sank. Had she really thought Nathan would set her mind at rest, telling her he knew for certain that there was nothing between Leo and Sonya Selby? But why should she care? If Leo was continuing his liaison with his girlfriend, she reflected, at least that kept him from making demands on her.

Leo had not returned home by the time Nathan called for her. Which meant she had had no opportunity of telling him where she was going.

'Vince Adley and his sister Caroline—you know them?' asked Nathan as they drove away from River Cottage. 'Of course you do,' he remembered, 'they were at your wedding. Vince was Leo's best man. They run this guesthouse, Moorview. They've got a big room they let us use for our craft meetings. This evening we'll just be a small group.'

Moorview was large, with a feeling about it that was as friendly and welcoming as its owners. Vince embraced Rhea as if he had known her all his life, while his sister took her hands, laughingly reminding her brother that Rhea was a married lady.

'Thanks for coming,' said Caroline.

'Thanks for inviting me,' Rhea answered, surprised and a little daunted by the interest and frank curiosity in the other people's faces.

'It's not often,' Vince declared loudly, 'that we get a real live professional in our midst.'

'Vince, you're embarrassing Rhea,' Caroline protested. 'Come and sit with me,' she added. 'And I'm known to my friends as Carrie. Have a coffee, and a biscuit. Go on, be a devil—they're home-made.'

As Rhea chewed appreciatively, a young woman asked from across the room, 'Is it true you've got a degree in art?'

'Applied art, specialising in textiles,' Rhea amended, somewhat startled by the efficiency of the village grapevine.

'I told them, Rhea,' Nathan explained. 'Hope you don't mind.'

'Don't let it put you off,' Rhea answered, laughing. 'I bet I'm no more skilled in my line than all of you are in yours.' She looked around the semi-circle of bright, friendly faces. 'What do you all do?'

'Come on now,' Vince ordered in a joking, military voice, 'confess by numbers. And introduce yourselves while you're about it.'

'I'm Maisie Kelney,' said a middle-aged lady. 'Leatherwork. And this is my daughter Joanie. She helps me.'

'Tommy Scott, clock restorer,' a bespectacled young man seated beside Joanie stated.

'Mildred Smith, and I make corn dollies.'

So the dozen people announced themselves and their crafts. They all held small samples on which they were working. The conversation became general and Nathan, seated on the other side of Rhea, refilled her cup.

Nathan crossed the room to continue his discussion with Tommy Scott and Carrie admired the piece of embroidery Rhea had brought along to work on.

'I'm a knitter, by hand, not machine,' Carrie told her. 'I find it relaxes me after a busy day caring for our guests. Would you...?' She hesitated, lowering her voice and colouring a little. 'I'd be delighted to knit anything you want, Rhea, in the way of outfits for the baby. Just make a list and——'

'Carrie!' Rhea had to cut her off. In an inexplicable way it hurt having to enlighten her. 'There's no baby coming. There never was.' Carrie's face fell, as Rhea had known it would. Hadn't even Nathan received the news with barely hidden disappointment? Not to mention Uncle Timmy. 'All the same, I really appreciate your offer.'

Carrie nodded, starting to speak, but changing her mind. The telephone rang on a table behind them, and Vince sprang to answer it, his eyes swinging to Rhea.

'Yes, Leo, your wife's here. Want to speak to her?'

Rhea's heart sank, having just caught the shout and the angry crash of metal on metal. Vince moved the receiver from his ear, his brows arched comically. Then he shook it and listened again, making a face and replacing it in its cradle.

'Oh, dear, one furious husband checking up on his wife's whereabouts. Didn't you tell him, Rhea?'

'Obviously not, Vince, and it's none of your business,' his sister reprimanded.

The evening passed too quickly for Rhea's liking. Not only was she enjoying the company of people who could, in a sense, speak her own language, but she couldn't forget Leo's minuscule, but none the less resounding explosion of anger.

When Nathan, taking her home, invited her in for a coffee first, half of her wanted to accept his invitation. The other, more sensible half, however, made her shake her head. 'I'd better get back,' she said.

'OK, another time,' he answered understandingly.

Leo's explosion on the telephone was nothing compared with his anger as she entered the front door. Furious and formidable, he stood in the doorway of the living-room, his shirt unbuttoned and pulled free as if he hadn't been able to bear its constriction. Since it was necessary to go through the living-room on her way to the kitchen, Rhea had no choice but to draw a deep, steadying breath and face Leo's anger.

CHAPTER SEVEN

REMINDING herself that the best form of defence, or so they said, was attack, Rhea made a pre-emptive strike.

'How could I tell you,' she challenged, her brown eyes flashing, 'when you weren't here?'

Leo thrust a thumb in the direction of the telephone. 'There was that.'

'That's true, and it did actually occur to me to call you, but I told myself you wouldn't care where I went or if I never came back. And don't deny it,' her voice rose accusingly, 'when you know it's true.' His anger seemed to be increasing with her every word, but she overrode a warning voice and plunged on, 'You're never here. When you are, you treat me as if I don't exist.'

Stop! her better judgement urged. You're as good as telling him you care, which you don't, you don't... Useless trying to stop now she had started.

'Day after day,' she went on, 'evening after evening, you take yourself off to the forge. Your uncle Timmy was right when he said you were obsessed with black-smithing. Or is it the most effective way you know of getting away from *me*? Or,' dared she? yes, she dared, 'maybe it's your *lady friend* you're obsessed with. Is it her you go to, not the forge? I bet she welcomes you each evening with open arms, which you go into without a single hesitation, a single qualm——'

One stride and he had seized her by the upper arms.

'Accusing me of adultery, are you?' he snarled, his eyes spitting like the forge fire. 'Because, if so, put it in writing, and I'll sue the hide off you!'

108

'That's right,' she cried wildly, struggling in vain to free her arms from the clamp of his fingers, 'talk like a true Dower! Take people's money away from them, leave them with nothing. Ask your wonderful brother what I'm talking about. As for you and your extra-marital activities——'

He slammed her against him. Jaw thrust forward, he ground out, 'So you'd rather my activities were *intra-marital*? That's OK by me, lady. Lead the way to your bedroom. No, on second thoughts, why waste time making the journey? Over here,' moving her towards the settee, 'will do very nicely. A little farewell get-together, before I leave.'

'Leave?' she asked, closing her eyes to hide her anxiety. 'You're—leaving?'

'Not for good, dear wife,' he rasped, 'although no doubt you're disappointed to hear it. On business, to London. But don't let your hopes rise. I'll be back. And demanding *this*, like any man in his right mind who's been parted from his *beloved*.'

He held her from him far enough for his hands to jerk her cotton top over her head, pull down the straps of her bra and, despite her gasps and protesting cries, fasten his mouth with a relentless, erotic possession over her burgeoning breasts.

Urging her backwards on to the sofa, he came down on top of her, the muscled weight of him robbing her of breath, the touch of his hands and sensual movement of his lips inflaming her and robbing her of any wish to repulse him.

On the contrary, she wanted—she actually wanted—to enfold him in her arms, stroke his hair, arch against him, whisper his name. She heard her own voice murmuring it, felt her own body slowly succumbing...heard the screech of the telephone splintering the tension and cooling the white-hot atmosphere to zero.

Leo's head lifted, and with a curse he broke contact and picked up the telephone, his other hand running through his hair. Rhea pulled on her cotton top and hated herself for her impassioned response to Leo's love-making. Except, she told herself, that 'love' hadn't come into it. She couldn't *love* a man she hated. Could she?

'Yes?' Leo barked into the phone. He listened, frowned and rapped out, 'Where the hell are you now?'

Dismayed, Rhea sank on to the sofa, guessing the identity of the caller. Agitatedly, she picked up and shook the cushion which still bore the imprint of their two heads.

Leo must have activated the voice amplifier, since Jerome's answer came over clearly. 'Now that'd be telling.'

'Cut that out, Jerome. You can't spend the rest of your life wandering the world.' Leo rubbed his chest hair abstractedly. 'What are you running away from?'

'Has she been talking?' There was a trace of anxiety in the question.

'She?' Leo asked coldly.

'My ex-fiancée, now your wife. I heard via the grapevine that you married her. So how are you liking her—er—charms, pal? As much as I did? I taught her a thing or two.'

Jerome burst out laughing, and Rhea clapped her hands over her ears. It's not true, she wanted to cry, but Jerome was talking again.

'I expect you know by now,' he went on as if he were enjoying himself, 'about her non-existent pregnancy. Caught you nicely, didn't she? Or did she own up *before* marriage, but, being the gentleman you are, and—er—because of what she told you, you kept your promise and got spliced to her all the same? One thing I know, you wouldn't have married her for love. Still,' in an amused, throwaway tone, 'you can always divorce her, can't you, when the time's right?'

'Both brothers,' Rhea exclaimed, unable to stay silent any longer, 'tarred with the same brush! Unscrupulous, manipulating——'

'What's she saying? Never mind,' Jerome remarked blandly, 'I guess she's kept quiet about—um—certain things; otherwise you'd be jumping down my throat by now. *Ciao*, brother, *sweet* sister-in-law.'

The call was cut with a clatter. Leo turned, hands in pockets, head slightly lowered. 'What things?' he asked.

I won't be intimidated, Rhea vowed. There's no one in the whole world now who'll stand up for me except myself.

'You're not interested in my past history,' she answered boldly. 'I drifted into your life temporarily, and I'll drift out of it *permanently*. As your brother said, you can divorce me when the time's right.'

'Stop prevaricating and answer my question.'

'How do I know,' her eyes defied him, 'that you aren't in league with him? Look how neatly you both had that business of his women tied up. He played around with them, then he sent them to you to pay them off.'

'So?'

'So how do I know you weren't his partner in crime?'

'What crime?'

Even now she could hardly bring herself to talk about it. 'I'm surprised you don't know. But then he wouldn't have told you, would he? Wanting to keep on the right side of his big brother. You were, after all, the one who got him out of his woman troubles.'

He stood in front of her now, arms folded, legs firmly placed. The rest of him towered. Tall as he was, he made the ceiling seem low. He waited with a false patience, his face unreadable in the subdued glow from the table lamp.

'I——' She looked at him, looked away.

'Take your time. We've got all night.'

All night? How would she sleep after what had taken place between them before the phone rang? Then her mind played over the events of the past, resentment returning. Why should she have a guilty conscience over marrying Leo out of revenge? Especially on the terms he had set out as a basis for their 'marriage'. Surely she had deserved some form of reparation for what Jerome had done to her family, her life.

And telling Leo the truth didn't mean he would believe her. Remember, she told herself, he's a Dower, and the Dowers stick together regardless. Not once during Jerome's calls had Leo got really angry with him. Which surely proved—didn't it?—that he was on his brother's side, always had been and always would be, judging by what Uncle Timmy had told her about their past.

'Why shouldn't I have sought payment for what Jerome did to my life?' The bitter words came tumbling from her of their own accord. 'Why shouldn't I have sought revenge for the way he behaved——?'

'You distinctly told me,' Leo interrupted, frowning, 'that Jerome hadn't made you pregnant.'

'Which was true. It's his fraud I'm talking about, his fraudulent activities.'

'*Fraud*?'

'Yes, *fraud*. And theft.' She leaned forward, rubbing at her ankle, which still pained her, like the events of the past which just wouldn't let her rest. 'If I tell you, will you believe me?'

'Try me.' He joined her on the sofa, reclining, arms extended, head turned her way.

Rhea enlarged the space between them, while Leo watched the action with narrowed eyes.

She rubbed her neck, which had begun to ache with tiredness, pushed a distracted hand through her hair. 'Jerome wangled a high position in the family firm——'

'Daniel Hirst?'

She nodded. '—by becoming engaged to me. Liking Jerome—he had his charms,' she admitted wryly, 'and seeing him as his future son-in-law, my father trusted him implicitly. Jerome abused that trust.'

Rhea stole a glance at Leo, seeing his half-closed eyes and wondered if he was asleep. 'Are you listening?' she thrust into the silence.

'He betrayed that trust, you were saying. How?'

He was, she realised, fully alert, watching her face, her mouth, her every agitated action.

'No doubt you won't believe me, and Jerome would deny it yet again if he heard me.' She sighed, recalling every unhappy detail. 'I'll tell you, all the same. Slowly but surely he bled the firm's finances dry. He not so much pocketed the company's money as moved it in shovelsful, into an account with an overseas bank.'

Leo was listening now. He got to his feet, walked up and down.

'No one,' Rhea went on, eyes closed, seeing the past so clearly it hurt, 'no one ever discovered how much, or where, or how he did it, and he wasn't telling. He denied everything, as his legal adviser told him to do. The money was never recovered.'

Leo stood at the window, staring into the darkness.

'I was left with the private mess, the public debts,' she said. 'Only when everything had been sold that could be sold, the house, the paintings my father had bought, all his investments cashed, his savings swallowed up, was I able to settle those debts.'

'You were left with nothing?'

'Not even anywhere to live. All my worldly goods I carried in the cases and backpack I took with me. They're up there now,' she gestured overhead, 'in the room you've allowed me to occupy.'

Leo broke the long silence. 'Until Jerome came on the scene and started to do as you've just alleged he did——'

There it was again, the doubt, the 'Jerome could do no wrong' attitude of his. *Alleged*, he'd said, not proven, as the judiciary had decided, letting Jerome off; Jerome, who had been so clever, allowed to walk free, able to keep his money, free of all responsibility for the company's demise.

'Until then,' Leo was saying, 'the company, Daniel Hirst, was thriving?'

'No—I did tell you. It started going downhill just before Jerome joined the firm. Which is why my father was so eager to appoint him. His son-in-law-to-be, filling the place of the son he'd never had—he was delighted with my *wonderful* fiancé, he trusted him implicitly. He'd save the firm, my father said, with his new, young ideas.'

He must have heard the bitterness, but he did not comment.

'Even if Jerome had been honest,' Rhea went on, 'it wouldn't have worked. The customers who had patronised Daniel Hirst so faithfully in the past noted the new direction the firm was taking and expressed their annoyance by drifting away. The young people didn't turn up in their droves as my father had hoped, and the slide down became an avalanche.'

'On whose recommendation did your father appoint Jerome?'

'His own. He produced his own CV, forged his own references. A pack of lies, as I found out later, after my parents had died—at least Dad was spared that. Jerome had made up his own qualifications, his "past experience" in management and finance. They were all phoney.'

There was another long silence, giving Rhea time to reflect. Recalling the past and talking about it brought it all back. It had stirred up all the bitterness and rancour she had felt when it was all over and Jerome had walked away, leaving her with nothing but his brother's address and a promise of payment on demand.

'So now do you see,' she challenged, 'why I vowed to get my own back on the Dowers in whatever way I could?'

Leo came to stand in front of her, tall and broad, eyes glacier-cold.

'And that way was handed to you on a plate, wasn't it? By me. OK, you've been through a hard time, I accept that, but what I can't find it in myself to forgive is your ruthless decision to use me as if you had really been expecting Jerome's child. Used me,' he pulled her up to stand in front of him and she quivered inwardly under the lash of his anger, his blazing eyes, 'deviously, as a weapon of revenge, to hit back at Jerome for all the harm he did you.'

'And my family,' she put in swiftly.

'A big debt, wasn't it, to seek reparation for? For which *I* paid. OK, so I'll pay in my own way, by keeping my promise to fund you while you bear my name and live in my house...but also by making *you* pay—for your ultimate freedom from me.'

'But you promised!' she cried, hearing the threat and guessing its meaning.

'That promise,' he released her arms with a jerk that shook her, 'was made null and void when you confessed you weren't pregnant—I've already told you that. From now on, Rhea, as far as our relationship's concerned, *I'll* be the one who calls the tune. Do you understand?'

White now, and reeling inside under the impact of his words, Rhea went slowly to the door. If he ever made love to her, slept with her *no holds barred*, as he had threatened, she would never be able to hide from him her true feelings, her need of him, both physically and mentally. She realised again how reckless she had been in using Leo Dower as her means of revenge.

'Thank you,' she said, turning, 'for giving me a roof over my head, temporary though it is. And for listening to me. And for believing me.'

He made a cut-off movement, but she climbed the stairs, too weary and too dispirited to take any more of his anger that night.

Rhea filled the days of Leo's absence by concentrating on her work. Mrs Litton continued to come twice weekly, and complained that there was hardly anything for her to do.

'You've done it all, Mrs Dower. And you're ever so much easier to tidy up after than your husband.'

Rhea laughed, wondering what Mrs Litton would say if she told her, 'I know hardly anything of my husband's ways. We live separate lives…and it's getting me down.' The thought escaped her control like a wild animal breaking free of its cage.

It isn't, she told herself frantically, it's what I want until we finally part. I'm *not* missing him. I *mustn't* become involved with the man I married, either emotionally or in any other way. What's more, I won't, she decided, switching her attention to her work. I'll carry on keeping him at a distance. I won't even *think* about him.

All the same, he intruded on her thoughts, and even had the temerity to appear in her dreams. Sometimes, rather than let him into her sleeping hours, she would fling out of bed and reach for her work, pieces of which littered her room.

Evenings were the hardest part, when she was tired and fed up with her own company. When Nathan rang a week into Leo's absence, inviting her to join the crafts group at the Dog and Badger, she jumped at the idea.

'I'd like to put a suggestion to you,' he said, but did not elaborate. 'I'll be round in ten minutes.'

'I'd rather walk there, honestly,' Rhea assured him. 'It's a beautiful evening, and I love the exercise.'

With some reluctance she turned her back on the moorland that stretched into the far distance, green and brown and golden in the setting sun, and opened the door of the pub.

Shouts of welcome greeted her from the dimness of the interior, the low wooden beams causing even Rhea to lower her head a little.

' "When the cat's away",' Timmy's joking voice came out of the shadows. 'Hello, lass. Missing your other half?'

'Yes, I am.' The admission came off the top of her head, she told herself firmly, not from her heart. Nathan patted the empty space he had saved and she eased her slender frame into it. Carrie sat at his other side.

Timmy laughed at Rhea's uncensored admission, plainly believing it. He swallowed the contents of his glass and thumped it down on the bar counter where he stood. 'I'll tell him, that I will,' he promised, patting her shoulder as he passed her on the way to the door.

'Please don't,' she pleaded, but her words were lost in the general hubbub.

'Glad you could make it,' remarked Carrie, leaning forward and talking across Nathan.

'Good to see you,' commented Nathan, his eyes appreciating her scarlet cotton sweater and matching trousers. Flattering to my ego, Rhea considered, but perhaps just a little too appreciative for a comfortable friendship. Carrie's bright gaze told of a touch of envy, and maybe a trace of jealousy? Or is it my imagination? Rhea wondered.

Vince, who had been chatting to the girl behind the bar, placed a drink in front of Rhea. 'It's alcoholic. You're not on the wagon, I hope, as well as virtually living in purdah?' was his joking comment as he put the glass in front of her. 'All creative artists such as we are,' everyone pretended to bow, 'need to come out into the world now and then to recharge their imaginative batteries. Tell that husband of yours to open the door of your gilded cage and throw away the key.'

Rhea joined in the laughter, but she knew how mistaken Vince was to think that Leo actually wanted to *keep* her. She had no doubt that the greatest moment of his life would be when she walked out of his cottage for the last time.

'Have you heard,' Carrie asked, capturing Rhea's attention eagerly, 'about the craft show we're putting on next month in the town? We've hired a hall with an entrance on to the main street.'

'We've done it before,' Nathan put in, 'and it's been a roaring success. We charge a small entrance fee, put a notice outside and sit back and wait for the custom.'

'We usually do well, get a lot of interest from the townspeople and tourists alike.'

'Would you like to exhibit?' enquired Vince, getting up to buy more drinks. 'We'd reserve a stall for you.'

Rhea, who had been smiling from one to the other, nodded happily. This camaraderie, this sharing of interests, was something she had never known in the life she had left behind. 'I'd love to,' she answered simply, and watched as Carrie made a note of the date and place, passing the scrap of paper to her.

Nathan reached into a bag at his side. 'This is the other thing I wanted to talk to you about,' he said, producing a couple of items of pottery he had made. 'These are plain and simple, straight from the hand of the potter. But it occurred to me that——'

'You'd like me to add some colour?' asked Rhea, comprehending at once. 'Decorate them, in other words?' The kind of thing your wife used to do? she almost added, but thought better of it. Nathan wouldn't want to discuss his personal affairs in public.

'Or otherwise adorn them, yes. Would you be willing?' he asked eagerly. 'To collaborate, I mean?'

She handled the pottery, admiring its lines, considering Nathan's proposition. 'It would be a new venture for me,' she admitted with a smile, 'but yes, I'd love to have a go.' She frowned. 'The trouble is, I don't have a workplace, only the——' She checked herself quickly. She had been about to say, 'only where I sleep', telling the world that she and Leo did not share a room!

'Not even a table,' she filled in hurriedly, 'to mess around on with my batik.' She felt she'd said enough. Much more and she might be giving away the true state of affairs between herself and Leo.

'There's a——' Nathan stopped himself too, realising that they could be overheard by other customers.

'I could clear a table in my workroom for you,' Mildred Smith offered. 'It's only covered in bits and pieces for my corn-dolly work.'

'That's very nice of you, Mildred,' Rhea acknowledged.

'No, no,' Nathan intervened, 'I was going to say that there's a spare area in my studio that I could let you have. You've seen it, Rhea. You remember it? You could make as much mess with your batik or whatever as you liked. Also, you'd be on the spot if there was any decision to be made, such as colour and so on. There's a folding bed in the room too, if you ever want to work too late to go home.' Here Vince whistled loudly and shook his head in mock disapproval. Nathan caught Rhea's hand. 'How about it?'

He was so excited that Rhea would have found it difficult to refuse even if she'd wanted to. 'Wonderful! Fine by me,' she answered, her eyes shining. 'Just as long as you don't mind my mess.'

'Shake on it, pal.' And they did, Nathan holding her hand just a little longer than necessary.

'Hi, there,' said Vince to the couple who had just entered. The man, who was tall, dark and business-suited, ducked to avoid the low beams. 'Your wife's being seduced by a friend of yours.'

Leo's eyes were cold as they rested on Rhea's flushed face. She could not hide her pleased surprise at his return,

until she saw the woman at his side. So that was why
Sonya had been missing from the village in the last few
days! She had been with Leo in London.

Ice, as cold as Leo's appraisal, began to form around
her heart. She told herself she should have known that
Leo's relationship with his girlfriend was still on the
agenda, despite his marriage. After all, it was an empty
marriage, which was how she wanted it, she told herself,
so why should she feel as if she wanted to cry?

'How did you know where to find Rhea?' asked
Carrie, glancing uncomfortably at Nathan's hand which
was still linked with Rhea's.

'I met my uncle Timmy, and he told me my wife was
here. She was missing me, he said. It seems he was
wrong.' Leo's glacial gaze moved from the half-filled
glass in front of Rhea to her hand which Nathan, for
some reason, refused to release.

Sonya's arm slipped through Leo's. 'My tongue,
darling,' she stage-whispered, 'it's dry as a bone!' She
nudged him towards the bar counter. He nodded briefly
and moved at her bidding.

She can have him, Rhea found herself thinking, he's
not mine, nor I his. To hide her agitation, she reached
out for Nathan's pottery that still stood on display,
running her fingers over it. Her eyes slid of their own
accord to the two figures at the bar. Sonya was in conversation with an acquaintance, but, to Rhea's profound
shock, Leo was leaning back against the counter, drink
to his lips, eyes narrowly and assessingly on her, his wife.
She shivered under that implacable, faintly lecherous
regard, sure that he was mentally undressing her, layer
by layer, until he laid bare not only her naked self, but
her most private thoughts, her very soul.

One day, she knew for certain, he would make it his
business to break down the invisible barrier between them
and, coldly but relentlessly, make her his—hadn't he said
as much?—if only to prove his domination over the

woman in her. What frightened her most was that, no matter how many times she told herself she hated him, that woman in her wanted his lovemaking with a piercing longing that was slowly but surely eating away at her equilibrium, her very peace of mind. But, she vowed, when that time did come, she would fight him every inch of the way.

CHAPTER EIGHT

'ANOTHER drink, please, darling,' Sonya was saying, and Leo, turning his back on the assembled company, but most of all, Rhea felt, on herself, obliged.

She wasn't consciously intending to leave, but her legs made their own decision, pushing back the chair. Taking leave of her friends, she made for the door.

Nathan, following her example, left with her. 'I'll take you home,' he offered, leading the way to his car.

'Thanks, but I think I'll take a walk. I need...' 'to get away', she had been going to say, but amended it to '...the exercise.'

Nathan looked worried. 'At this time of night?'

Rhea looked at the clear blue sky, splashed across with sunset colours. 'It won't be dark for a while. I'll be OK.'

Still anxious but respecting her wishes, Nathan drove off with a wave.

Alone, Rhea shivered as the cool of the evening penetrated her thin jacket and plain cotton trousers, but the lower temperature did not deter her. She did need to get away, to sort herself out, her thoughts, her feelings.

Soon the straggling line of cottages ended, the road climbing up on to the moors. Rhea loved the sweeping line of them, tracing the gentle slopes as they lifted to meet uneven escarpments rising high and, as daylight faded, menacingly in the near distance.

This was a beauty, a freedom which a town dweller such as she had always been knew nothing about. To live among these for the rest of her life with a man she loved—she would ask for nothing more. Her subconscious mind made a correction...*the* man she loved. No, no, she disputed it, she loved no man, *no man*. How could she, after the man she thought had loved her had treated her and her family so badly?

Leaving even the drystone walls behind, she trod the springy surface of the moors themselves, straying from the road, lost in the past. Deciding to rest, she sank down on to the hard, tussocky ground, leaning back on her hands. Pictures arose, and sounds from the past, superimposing themselves over the intense peace and beauty around her. She lay full length and closed her eyes.

'My dad and my mother!' she had shrieked, throwing open the door of Jerome's office in the heart of London. 'The police came to see me at work. Oh, Jerome, Jerome, my parents, they're——' she could hardly get the words out '—the policewoman told me—they're dead!'

She had rushed to his side as he had sat at his desk, grasping his arm and shaking it. 'For God's sake, Jerome, tell me it's a bad dream, that it isn't true!'

Jerome had risen, looking at her with horror and something very like fear. 'Of course it's not true.' He had glanced at his watch. 'They've reached the South of France by now. Your dad's an experienced pilot, he'd take all the necessary precautions about landing, following all the instructions from ground control. The police have just got the wrong name, that's all.'

He had satisfied himself, but not Rhea. She'd shook her head madly, sick with anguish, bewildered by the attitude of the man she was going to marry. 'They're dead, I tell you!' she'd cried. 'The police wouldn't make that kind of mistake. They gave me a description of his plane and its number, and they're all correct.'

Instead of his arm going round her shoulders, it had reached out to the telephone. A call or two later, during which Rhea had stood trembling at his side, he'd replaced the phone slowly and looked at her with anxious, and strangely wary eyes.

'It's true,' he'd told her. 'They crashed as they approached the Channel. Your dad must have realised something was wrong. He'd made for some woods, obviously hoping to soften the landing, but it didn't.' He'd paused, then in a deadpan voice added, 'I'm sorry to hear it, Rhea. My deepest condolences.'

'Is that all you've got to say? You don't care, do you? Either for me or about them!' she had accused. 'If you did, you'd be holding me, comforting me, telling me you'd see to everything. For heaven's sake, Jerome, you're going to be *my husband*!' she had cried. 'You've told me you love me. I believed you, Jerome, but now I—I'm beginning to wonder...'

'Hush,' he'd soothed, his arm around her now but more brother than lover, 'you're being hysterical. It'll all come right, you'll see.'

She had drawn away from him then, in horror. 'All come right?' she had shrieked. 'When my parents are *dead*? How can you be so unfeeling?' She had stared at him as a terrible thought had occurred. 'You never did what you'd promised to do, did you? You didn't do a single thing about——'

The sound of a car on the moorland road nearby broke into her nightmare thoughts. If I lie still, she thought, wiping away the tears that just wouldn't stop coming, the driver won't see me. But it seemed the driver had, apparently spotting her even in the darkness that had hidden the moors as she had been lying there, leaving only their outline beneath a clear turquoise sky and the rising moon to see by.

Her heart pounded as a tall, unmistakably masculine figure loomed in the semi-darkness, striding, angry, standing over her. It took no more than two seconds for her to recognise him, but her heartbeats speeded up rather than slowed.

He must have contacted Nathan, believing him to have taken her home, discovering from him not only her intention to go for a walk, but the direction she had taken. So what, she thought, if he had come to find her? It meant absolutely nothing. It was in his own interests to find her, wasn't it? A missing wife, lost on the moors at night through his negligence, as others would see it, would sit sorely on his conscience.

'*Sunbathing*?' was his caustic comment as he watched her sit up and shake her long hair to free it of pieces of last year's heather. 'Or should I coin a phrase and call it moonbathing? What the hell are you doing here? Are you so suburban-minded, so ignorant of country ways as to think it's safe to come up on to the moors in the late evening, on foot, alone, without adequate clothing or footwear or a torch?'

'Why should you care?' she challenged, rubbing her damp cheeks with the back of her hand. 'I'm just an encumbrance to you. I married you under false pretences, remember? If I lay here all night and died of exposure, no doubt you'd be glad——'

He reached down and secured her wrist in a grip of iron, pulling her to her feet. 'Don't play with me, lady, don't provoke me, or you might get more than you——'

He saw her wince. 'What's wrong?' Dumbly, she pointed to her foot, and he flashed a torch down. 'For pity's sake, you've hurt it again?' She nodded. Then the torch beam showed him her tear-stained face. 'It hurts that much?' She shook her head. 'So what have you been crying over? Or should I say who? Sorry now you married me and therefore aren't free to pursue your relationship with Nathan Oxley?'

'That's ridiculous! He's OK, he's a nice man, but——'

'So who caused those tears?' Hooded eyes fixed on her face. 'Don't tell me, let me guess. Jerome.'

It was so true that she found herself nodding, realising too late just how he would interpret the admission.

'So,' his lips thinned, 'although he let you down, treated you abominably, you're still missing him, are you, missing his arms, his lovemaking?'

He disregarded her fiercely shaking head. His arms lifted to encircle her waist, wrapping her so tightly to him that she had to struggle for breath. His mouth was so near to hers that she felt its movement as he talked. 'Don't fret, my lovely. I've already taken his place in your life, so I'll take his place in your bed. And,' he moved her slightly to one side, 'what better bed than the moorland we're standing on?'

'Leo, please don't. I know you're only fooling, but——'

'And that's where you're wrong, my heart.' A beautiful endearment, but so cynically spoken. 'I'm deadly serious. We're entirely alone. Few people come up here in the darkness. And even if we're seen, a man and woman lying together, people would jump to the usual conclusion—in this case, the correct conclusion. So no one will disturb us.'

She tried again. 'Leo, not now, not here. Not *ever*. It would be a meaningless act.' She was frightened now, by the look on his face, the cold intent in his eyes as they gleamed in the moonlight.

He bent her slowly, and, although she stiffened to resist the pressure he was imposing on her much frailer frame, her knees buckled and she found herself lying beneath him. The woman in her leapt with joy to find that this man, at last, was where often in her dreams she had imagined him. But her reason cried, Hold him off, stop him somehow...

Summoning all her strength, she twisted and turned, flailing with her legs, even managing to bite his hand as it held her face still.

'Little bitch,' he hissed, lowering his twisted lips and covering hers with them in a kiss that robbed her of any strength she had left. His mouth, merciless in its intent, worked at hers until they parted, allowing him all the access he was demanding.

Somehow his hand had found its way inside her cotton top, capturing a breast and fastening punishingly over it, then miraculously gentling, moulding, moving across to stroke the other. His change of tactics was almost her undoing, and his mouth absorbed her shuddering breaths, his tongue discovering her inner sweetness, his free hand lifting to caress her throat.

'Did Jerome do this to you?' his lips asked against hers. 'Did he get through your defences, take what he wanted, as he did with all the others? And like them, did you give him all he asked and more? Did you fight him like you're fighting me?'

'Yes—no.' He was giving her a breathing-space, one which her dazed but still rational mind told her to take but which her emotions didn't want. The fight was within herself now, and she was torn in two.

Anger came to her rescue, and provided her with the ammunition with which to return his fire. 'While you were away,' she spat, 'did you do this to Sonya Selby? Did you share a hotel room and make love to her every night?'

Slowly Leo loosened his hold, staring into her moon-washed face, his expression dark and unfathomable. He rolled on to his side, lying back, a hand cushioning his head. If Rhea had expected a denial, she was bitterly disappointed.

'If I did, what of it? Our marriage is barren, that you can't deny. Look at your response to me just now. I married a frigid woman, didn't I, Rhea Hirst?'

'No!' Her denial was like the cry of a wounded animal. 'I'm not that, I'm not!'

'You're *cold*, you're *frigid*,' Jerome had accused, shifting away from her petulantly in the car, on the sofa in the sitting-room while her parents had slept. 'It wouldn't even be any good undressing you and taking you to bed. To function as a man, I like a woman with fire, who spits and scratches, then throws herself at me. My God,' he would get up, stare disgustedly down at her, 'it wouldn't even be any good, would it, softening you up with alcohol? You'd just get drunk and fall into bed—alone. What did I get myself engaged to you for?'

She hadn't known then, but she subsequently and excruciatingly had learned that particular answer. Yet here was another Dower brother making the same accusation, calling her unresponsive and cold...when with all her heart and soul she longed to make love with him, join with him in a true and lasting and *loving* relationship. Yet the very terms of their marriage precluded that. They'd married for expediency, nothing else.

She hadn't really loved Jerome—she'd realised that long before the final split. Puzzled by her own inhibited reactions to the man she called her fiancé, she had wondered if the fault lay with her own personality. She started to compare her relationship with Jerome with the one that existed between her parents.

There had been no mistaking that they had loved each other, from the way they'd caught each other's eye, hugged each other on the spur of the moment, even held hands sometimes while walking. Yet it had taken three cataclysmic events in her life to wake her up to the truth—that she didn't love Jerome, never had, never would. Nor did he love her.

Rhea walked beside Leo to the car parked at the roadside. Her ankle still hurt a little, but she was darned if she was going to tell him.

Preoccupied, he moved slightly ahead, then turned, noticing her plight. 'What's wrong? Old trouble come back?' She nodded, shrugging it off. When she was level with him, he placed a supporting arm around her waist.

'I'm all right, thanks,' was her snapped response, but his hold only tightened.

'Much more and I'll carry you,' he clipped.

At once Rhea tolerated his help. If he picked her up, she wouldn't be able to stop herself clinging to him, wouldn't be able to resist the attraction which his own particular aroma had for her, couldn't stop her cheek from nestling against his shoulder.

What am I going to do, she asked herself as she lay in bed later in the dark silence, about this love for Leo Dower that's taken such firm hold inside me that I know I'll never be able to uproot it and replace it with love for any other man on earth?

Finding no answer, she twisted and turned, unable to rest. Her watch told her that two hours had passed since Leo had left her at the door of his office.

'You're starting work,' she had asked him, 'at this time of night?' Then she realised how 'wifely' the question must have sounded.

'That was my intention,' he answered, leaning against the door-frame, in his eyes the coolly indolent look with which he had regarded her through the semi-darkness and smoky atmosphere of the pub. 'Why, have you got a better idea?'

She knew what he meant and cursed herself for inadvertently providing the encouragement he had plainly detected in her innocent question. But had it truly been innocent? she asked herself as she fled up the stairs. Of course it had, she told herself. In fact, the sooner the door was closed between her and his mocking amusement the better.

Switching on the bedside lamp, she flung out of bed. Standing at the window and staring into the darkness, she forced herself to face the fact that the woman in her, having been awoken from her long sleep in those passionate moments on the moors, was not only refusing stubbornly to return to her slumbers, but was threshing about demanding to be noticed and pandered to—by the man who cared nothing for her, but who had so carelessly and so implacably aroused that femininity, not in love, nor even affection, but in anger and cynical retribution.

She would do some work, she decided—no, better than that, she would assemble and pack everything she would need in order to do her work at Nathan's place. As she piled brushes and cutting tools and pieces of fabric into a suitcase, she heard the creak of a floorboard.

Freezing with a primitive kind of fear, she listened. The door-handle turned and, with agitated hands, she pressed the contents more firmly into the bulging case and lowered the lid. Springing to her feet, hiding the telltale case, she faced the newcomer.

He entered slowly, staring at her with a look that set her pulses racing. She tugged ineffectually at the neckline of her fine lawn nightdress, aware that against the light it was semi-transparent, and reproached herself for not having had the forethought to pull on a robe.

'We have, I think you'll agree,' he said, his eyes carrying out a leisurely reconnaissance of her outlined shape, 'some unfinished business to attend to, you and I.'

In the semi-darkness, he looked overpoweringly handsome. He wore creased denims that hugged his thighs and a navy cotton shirt from the opened neck of which sprang a patch of curling hair which matched in colour the evening's growth of stubble.

All Rhea's instincts were telling her to stay right where she was. Since she couldn't physically escape him—he stood, hands on hips, elbows jutting out, a barrier in themselves across the path to the door—she had no alternative but to keep him at bay with words.

'Unfinished business? I—I don't know what you mean,' she lied. 'I'm sure you finished your *business* activities to your complete satisfaction back there in London with Miss Selby.'

'Are you being deliberately obtuse?' Leo moved slowly towards her. 'Or maybe you're baiting me?'

One step, two... her feet took her backwards, away from him. She awarded them full marks for initiative, but they were out of phase with the rest of her body. The one thing in the world she did not want to do was run away.

'Because if you are, you'll get more than you bargained for. And,' he halted in front of her, 'if you don't stop looking at me as if I were something unpleasant from a waste-disposal site, I'll——'

'I'm not frigid, Leo.' Horrified, she heard the words burst from her. To his ears they must sound like blatant encouragement.

'You aren't? You know that for certain? You and Jerome——'

'Not Jerome!'

'You've had other men? This is getting interesting,' he responded, deeply sarcastic. 'Is my beautiful wife about to confess the secrets of her romantic past? Or,' his eyes gleamed, 'was it all so mechanical and *unro-mantic* that it turned you sexually cold?'

'What you're saying is pure invention on your part,' she declared. 'All the same, you—you mustn't make love to me, Leo.'

'*Mustn't?*' His brows drew ominously together. 'What is this? First you try and assure me you're not cold, which is come-on number one. Second, you stand there,' impatient fingers untied the bootlace shoulder-straps and eased the nightdress to waist level, 'telling me, your husband, that I *must not* make love to you, my wife? Did you honestly think,' now his palms caressed her milky-white breasts, and her eyes closed at the overwhelmingly pleasurable sensation he was creating, 'that ours would be a brother-and-sister relationship? Despite my warning that, sooner or later, I'd make you pay for using me as your means of revenge against Jerome?'

Leo didn't wait for an answer. He swept her into his arms and dropped her on to the bed, tearing off his shirt and throwing it aside. Bending over her, he made short work of removing her nightdress, tossing it to join his discarded clothing.

In his eyes as they surveyed her nakedness, search though she might, she could perceive no warmth and certainly nothing at all approaching love, only desire and sensuality, a feeding of his male appetite before swooping on his prey.

'Please,' she protested hoarsely, 'not like this! Not coldly and deliberately, as if I...as if I were——' She found she couldn't go on because to her dismay her voice had grown thick with tears.

For a fraction of a second, his eyes closed. He took a deep breath and let it out slowly. Rhea guessed he had put a brake on his own masculine reflexes, and experienced a rush of gratitude for the way he had answered her plea.

Discarding the rest of his clothes, he dropped beside her. He pulled her round until she was lying intimately against him and she felt the full impact of his aroused masculinity. With his forefinger he wiped away the tears that had escaped from beneath her eyelids.

He ran his palms over her tingling skin, wound his legs around hers and lowered his head to suckle and tease at her hardened breasts. Her fingers dug into the muscles of his upper arms and her throat opened on a shuddering gasp.

His head came up and he covered her parted lips with his probing mouth, exploring deeply until her body tensed with a desire that had nothing whatsoever to do with revenge or retribution and everything to do with taking and giving and loving.

His lips moved down, following a tantalising trail around her ears and down her throat, where her breasts caused a fiery diversion. He suckled and nipped alternately until she could hardly breathe for the pleasure he was giving her. On the trail again, his breath created a heated path down, down to places that throbbed unbearably under the onslaught of his tongue, his hands joining in the piratical assault on her sexual sensibilities.

His head lifted, only to come up against the restraint of her hands gripping his hair—anything, she thought, to help her withstand those alien yet unbelievably pleasurable sensations he was arousing within her.

His head went down again and he imprisoned her lips in an erotic, delving kiss. Parting her thighs, he stroked and coaxed and eased an intimate path into the warm and pulsating essence of her. She gasped at his forced intrusion and he took her breath into him, pausing and, she sensed, restraining his own instincts, giving her time to accept him.

She felt his muscles tense beneath her curling fingers and his arousal of her began all over again. Taking his time now, with subtlety and a tingling excitation of her feminine responses, he touched and stroked and invaded the most secret areas of her writhing body, raising her desire and her passion to fever pitch.

At last her gasps and breathless cries of 'Oh, please, *please*,' must have drawn some mercy from him, since he took pity on her, at the same time giving free rein to his own driving male needs. Mindlessly and with a cry of pure delight she followed him every step of the way, soaring with him at last to a golden summit of wild and joyful fulfilment.

She awoke to an empty place beside her and the sound of water running. As she stirred and blinked, easing her luxuriously contented body and mind into gear, Leo appeared in the doorway, hair wet from the shower, a towel slung carelessly over his still damp shoulder, and wearing nothing else at all.

Rhea's heart jolted. Gazing at him, at his fit and virile body, the blatant masculinity that had swept her to a kind of earthly paradise only a few hours before, she felt her senses stir all over again.

He strolled to the bedside, pulling back the covering and looking down at her. She grew overwhelmingly conscious of her nakedness and, to his mocking amusement, colour suffused her cheeks as she gazed up at him.

'Now you know,' she remarked, using speech as a way of countering the almost unbearable desire he was arousing in her just by looking at her like that, 'that you were wrong in your accusation that I was frigid. I——'

'Poor Jerome! No wonder he——'

'He what?' she demanded, swinging her legs to the floor and seizing a wrap from a chair. 'The next time he phones, ask him, "Why didn't you take what an engaged man usually——?"'

'I'm asking you.'

'Do all your acts of lovemaking,' she challenged evasively, knowing the answer but not wishing to give it, 'end with your interrogating the woman who's allowed you to share her bed? For instance,' her eyes flashed fire, '"How many men have there been before me?" And, if she's virginal, "Why? Hasn't any man desired you enough to storm your defences?"'

He seized her wrists and forced them behind her. 'Any more insults, lady?' Her wrap fell open and he eased her backwards, his head lowering, his lips making free with her breasts. His arousal of her had started all over again.

His head so intimately near her, his deliberate onslaught on the still-tender flesh, made her want to push him away, but together they had an effect on her so potent that she forgot her vow of vengeance and felt herself longing to kiss the dark hair at his nape and the tanned skin of his neck.

He moved her back on to the bed, pushing her down and putting himself on top of her, and began to make love to her all over again. When the time came for him to repossess her, there was not an atom of resistance left inside her, and again she knew the sheer delight of erotic fulfilment, clinging to him and returning his kisses and glorying in the feel of the essence of him flowing into her.

A clock chiming somewhere in the house roused them, and he rolled from her, lifting her upright with him and kissing her deeply, holding her to him and staring into her radiant face.

Letting her go, he pulled the wrap around her throbbing body and picked up the towel, winding it round his waist. He took to wandering round her room, glancing at her possessions.

Secretly she watched him, his potent masculinity a magnet she was powerless to resist. She had never, until now, believed it possible to love one's enemy, but now she knew. She loved *this* enemy on whom she had sworn revenge for what his brother had done to her, she loved him with a strength that shook her to her very core.

He moved to leave, coming up against the suitcase into which she had been cramming her work. The catches were not fastened and the lid was propped half open.

Her heart nosedived as he stared down, pushing with his bare foot at the fabric spilling out. Slowly he turned, and Rhea saw that all indulgence, all warmth had been wiped away.

Narrowed eyes sliced into her. 'Thinking of leaving? Remember to give me an address for forwarding, won't you?'

Rhea shook her head. 'You've got it wrong, Leo. I'm not leaving. I—I meant to tell you. Nathan's offered me space at his studio where I can make as much mess as I like. I couldn't do that here in your cottage, and anyway you haven't got a room to spare, a room that's—that's suitable.'

Anger forked across his eyes, causing her to falter. 'And,' she went on, 'there's the lighting aspect to consider, not the artificial variety, but daylight...'

He approached with measured steps. 'Did you ask me?'

'For—for permission? Of course not. We're free agents, you said.' She brazened it out. 'That was the condition under which I married you. We agreed to live our separate lives——'

'Ask me,' Leo persisted as if she hadn't spoken, 'if such a room existed in this cottage?'

Where had the wonderful feeling gone, the togetherness, the sense of belonging to this man?

'No. Nathan made the offer, and I couldn't think of any reason why I should refuse.' Attack, her other self was urging, don't defend! 'But, Leo,' she pretended bewilderment, 'you surely aren't *jealous*?' She knew she was goading him by his indrawn lips, but she went recklessly on. 'Of Nathan Oxley? I might as well be jealous of Sonya Selby.' Accusingly, she added, 'I'd have greater reason to be, the way you go around with her, travel with her to your *business* appointments, come back with her and flaunt her as your woman at the local pub in front of all the villagers.' She had to stop, her heart was pounding so. At the look in his eyes, she wanted to turn and run, but pride kept her there.

He stayed silent, but she wished he had shouted, raged at her accusations, telling her she was wrong in her assumption that he and Sonya were lovers.

'J-Jerome was right about you,' she flung at him, irritated beyond words at his silent domination of the conversation, 'you take up with a woman, sleep with her, then, when you're tired of her, ab-abandon her. You two make a good pair, don't you? I'd—I'd begun to trust you, Leo, I don't know why. I thought you possessed a quality that was so much more dependable and trustworthy than your brother, that placed you head and shoulders above Jerome. But I was wrong, wasn't I?'

He did not deign to answer her questions. 'Since we're into character analysis,' his eyes castigated and at the same time raked with a sensual indolence her figure beneath the flimsy wrap, 'two can play at that. Let me rip *yours* to pieces. You lied to me.' He mouthed the accusation slowly and clearly.

'What about? The non-existent pregnancy?' she took him up. 'It was *your* invention, not mine.'

'But you played along with my assumption. You used it, me, as a means of gaining access to my bank account, to the comfort and security I could offer, to a return to the social and financial status that had eluded you since the break-up of your life as you knew it.'

'I——' She was shaking her head when the telephone rang.

'Who?' she heard Leo bark from his room. 'Nathan? Yes?' No friendly greeting ensued, just another bark that summoned her to the phone.

'Hi, Nathan. Collect me and my things? That's nice of you. Give me an hour and I'll be ready when you arrive.'

Replacing the receiver, she turned, defiance in her eyes, but Leo had gone. The cottage seemed to shake with the slamming home of the front door.

It took Rhea no time at all to settle down to her work in Nathan's studio. Carrie, who told her she was often in and out of Nathan's place, helped her unpack, placing her books and illustrated volumes on the shelves that Nathan had allotted to her.

Intrigued, Carrie and Nathan watched her arrange her assortment of equipment, smiling at the double saucepan which, she told them, she used for melting the wax she had bought from a specialist craft shop.

'I could have provided you with cooking facilities,' Nathan declared, puzzled by the appearance of an electric hotplate which Rhea told them was a vital part of her work.

'Thanks,' she said with a smile, 'but I like to keep my mess, like my tools, in one place.'

Carrie inspected the fabrics she had brought, the bundles of cotton, silk and linen. She pored over the batik designs which Rhea had sketched in a notebook.

'Would you make me a skirt some time?' she asked wistfully. 'These designs are all so unusual and attractive.' Rhea promised that she would.

It was easy, Rhea discovered, working with Nathan in the room. As he fashioned his models and shapes, he became so absorbed that it was as though sometimes she was there on her own. That first day, he showed deep interest in her work, listening to her explanations and watching as she worked, invading his kitchen with his permission, waxing the fabrics, then dyeing them to the shade she required.

He took her home and she told him she had felt happier that day than for a long time.

'Can I take you for a meal, Rhea?' he asked with a touch of wistfulness.

She thought of Leo, arriving home to an empty house—after last night, surely he would break his routine of working late at the forge and join her?

She shook her head. 'It's a nice thought, Nathan,' she answered, 'but——'

'Another time? OK.'

'What about Carrie? I'm sure she'd love to be spoilt for once.'

He shook his head. 'This time of the day, she's always busy waiting on her guests.' He drove off with a wave.

Pushing open the door, Rhea stopped in her tracks. Leo was there before her, and her heart leapt at the thought that their closeness last night had meant more to him than just a passing satisfaction of his masculine desires. But a glance across the room changed all that.

His girlfriend lounged on the sofa, a glass in her hand, her relaxed attitude boasting of a familiarity with Leo's cottage that put Rhea firmly in her place as an interloper and temporary resident. Her outfit was a slinky kind of trouser suit, exotic flowers grown large, splashed across a black background.

Then Rhea realised that Leo too was dressed as formally as his guest, which could only mean that they had a dinner date. How could she have thought that last night had meant anything to him, that the day away from her had for him seemed as long as it had for her? Just how foolishly romantic could she get?

If that, Rhea thought defiantly, swallowing her intense disappointment, is how he's playing it, so can I. She nodded briefly at Sonya, who looked somewhat put out at the touch of hauteur in her hostess's manner, said 'Excuse me' to Leo, who stood in front of the phone, and dialled.

Leo, whose hand also held a glass, watched the stabbing action, leaning back against the cabinet that held the telephone.

'Nathan?' Rhea asked, injecting a warmth into her voice that must have brought a smile to Nathan's face. 'That meal you offered me—does the invitation still stand?'

'You bet,' Nathan answered. 'How does the Black Bull strike you? OK, I'll make a booking and call for you. Half seven? Hey, Rhea, I'm sure the sun's rising instead of sinking. Will you have to report first to——?'

'My prison warder? No, Nathan,' with a murderous flash of the eyes at Leo, 'he doesn't consult me about his moves. Why should I consult him?' She disconnected with a crash and flung out of the room.

'Black Bull be darned,' Sonya was saying on an explosion of laughter. 'I could hear *Nathan* pawing the ground in anticipation! What's it like, darling, to have a rival in love?'

'First,' came Leo's rasping reply, 'you have to be in love to have a rival in it.'

His cynical statement was, Rhea thought, her lip quivering, like a well-aimed missile crashing against her back. And if she hadn't been so stupid as to leave the voice amplifier switched on, they wouldn't have heard Nathan's replies.

For Nathan's sake, Rhea smiled and talked animatedly throughout the meal. Since most of their discussion ranged around their crafts, it wasn't difficult to sound enthusiastic. What Nathan did not know was that half the time her mind was on Leo and Sonya. He's *my* husband, she found herself thinking. Yet he had gone off with another woman in front of her very eyes! From her bedroom window she had watched them leave, Sonya's arm clinging to Leo's.

Nathan took her home, returning her thanks with a kiss on the cheek. Rhea hadn't cared if Leo had been standing at the window, but her defiance was pointless. The cottage was empty.

She went to bed, but could not sleep. It's the old, old story, she thought bitterly, rejected wife hoping against hope that the husband she loved would come home to her after all. Why should I take it on the chin? she asked herself, irritable with tiredness and a terrible sense of rejection. Pulling on a gown, she ran upstairs and down, disconnecting all the telephone points. Even if he rang there would be no answer to his calls, and he could put whatever construction on that that he liked. Eventually she slept, dreaming that she lay in Leo's arms and that he whispered over and over again that he loved her.

She awoke to daylight and pouring rain, convinced that Leo had stayed the night with his girlfriend. He certainly hadn't returned home. His room was empty, and she stared at his undisturbed bed, feeling shattered inside.

CHAPTER NINE

THE telephone rang as Rhea reconnected it. It just had to be Leo. Her heart sank when she heard Nathan's voice.

'Like me to come and get you?' he asked. 'This weather——'

'The river level's risen,' she told him, telling herself to accept the fact that Leo had spent the night with his girlfriend. Theirs was that kind of marriage, wasn't it? 'I can see it from the bedroom window. Thanks for the offer of a lift. The answer's yes, please. Ready in half an hour.'

Uncle Timmy was munching lunchtime sandwiches at the Dog and Badger as she preceded Nathan into the bar. Her heart leapt, then dived. Leo wasn't with him. Lifting his tankard, Timmy didn't quite manage to hide his worried look at the sight of her coming in with Nathan so, while Nathan ordered, Rhea made straight for Timmy's table. But nothing, she decided firmly, would make her ask where Leo was. All the same, she couldn't help wondering...

Hanging Nathan's damp jacket, which she had taken from him, around the back of a chair, she divested herself of her own, swinging it across the back of her own chair.

'It's still raining,' she offered as a conversational opening.

Timmy nodded. 'Cats and dogs.' He lapsed into an uncharacteristic silence. He's still annoyed with me, Rhea thought, for spending my lunch-break with Nathan.

'I've been working hard,' she remarked as a way, she hoped, of setting his fears at rest. She smoothed her damp hair, then played with a beer-mat, jumping when Timmy's hand reached out for her own.

'I can see,' he said. 'Looks as if you've painted your hands as well as the canvas, or whatever it is you use.'

Rhea laughed and looked up gratefully as Nathan set a plate of sandwiches and a glass of fruit juice in front of her. 'Those colours are from the dyeing process,' she told Timmy. 'I'm working on a series of batiks for the craft fair.'

'Not long now,' Nathan supplied, tucking into his lunch.

'First you wax the fabric,' Rhea went on, doing likewise, 'then you dye it to the colour you want. Then it's drained and dried, and——'

'A craft fair, you say?' queried Uncle Timmy. 'I think I heard Leo mention it.'

'Is he contributing?' asked Nathan, pushing away his empty plate. 'That'll be the first time, if he is. Refill, Rhea? Timmy?' He made his way to the bar.

'Leo's back at the forge,' Timmy said. 'Working himself into the ground, he is. After completing those gates, and the celebration last night——'

'What celebration?' Rhea asked tautly.

'Why, the installation of the gates, lass. I thought you'd be there, as his wife, like. But Leo said you—er— well, had another engagement.' He glanced across at Nathan's back. 'Said you stalked out, nose in the air. Said you were an impudent, ungrateful little package, and for two pins he'd either put you across his knee, or——'

'Or divorce me.' Rhea, her face scarlet, shot to her feet, to the astonishment of the other customers.

'My dear lass,' Uncle Timmy extended a soothing hand, but she evaded it, 'you said it, not me, nor Leo.'

'Rhea, wait a minute,' Nathan, returning to the table, tried to reason, 'just calm down.'

Rhea ignored their pleading restraint. 'OK, so let him divorce me. Let him. What's more,' she hauled her jacket on, 'I'm going to tell him so. See you later, Nathan.'

She raced along the road towards the forge, oblivious of the pouring rain and the way her shoes were filling as they splashed in puddles. She didn't care if Sonya was there, she didn't care about anything except telling her husband he could go jump in the river.

Bursting in, she stopped short, her eyes confused by the switch from daylight to semi-darkness. Then they cleared and she saw that he wasn't there. But Sonya was.

'Hi.' She rose from a desk which was tucked away in a corner. 'Oh, it's you, Mrs Dower. If you're looking for your——' obviously the word was anathema to her tongue '—Leo, he's——' her hand waved vaguely '—gone home.'

'So what are you doing here?'

A slow smile spread across Sonya's face at Rhea's show of jealousy, and Rhea wanted to kick herself for handing that piece of juicy knowledge to Leo's girlfriend. 'Wouldn't you like to know?' Sonya drawled, and turned back to the desk, shuffling paper.

So, Rhea perceived, Sonya Selby provided the clerical help that she, his wife, hadn't even known he needed.

It was still pouring as she arrived, panting, at the door of River Cottage. She scoured the downstairs and was in the hall when Leo appeared on the landing, wearing only a towel fixed around his waist. A swift glance took in her panting, shivering body.

'What the hell——?' was his biting question.

She made short work of the stairs and put herself on his level, except that his height, in comparison with hers, always gave him the advantage.

'No, not *hell*, and certainly not *heaven*. If it were, you wouldn't figure in it,' she got out between gasps for breath. 'All I want to say is, if you want to start divorce proceedings, go ahead—I won't stop you. It's time I was on my way, anyhow. Our marriage has lasted quite long enough as far as I'm concerned. Too long, in fact.'

Folding his arms across the whipcord leanness of his midriff, he surveyed her surveying him. For the life of her she couldn't stop her eyes from gazing at his stubborn jawline, his broad shoulders, his expanse of chest. Fascinated, she saw the tiny beads of water from the shower he had clearly just taken, still clinging to his mat of chest hair.

'OK,' a muscle twitched in his cheek, 'so what's this all about?'

'You want a divorce, so it's the end, Leo.' The rain ran uncomfortably down her neck from dripping strands of hair.

'Who said?'

'Uncle Timmy over lunch.' He hadn't, she corrected herself, but he had had time, if he'd wanted to, to contradict her statement before she had rushed out. 'It's Sonya you want in your life, not me. She's at the forge now, working with you, and you want her living with you too. I could see that last night a mile off. You took her out for the evening.'

'A celebration. We finished the gates and they're fixed in place. It was a big order, and the customer gave a party. I'd have taken my wife, but she walked out on me into the arms of another man.'

'You had your girlfriend with you,' she flung back, 'don't try to deny it. So why shouldn't I use the freedom of our marriage arrangement and accept a *man* friend's invitation? What's more, you stayed the night with her. And you didn't even telephone to tell me you wouldn't be home.'

'Oh, yes, I did.' He moved closer, towering over her, his stance intimidating, his bearing, his muscular solidity almost irresistible to Rhea's inflamed senses. 'Three times I tried, but no reply. You were out, at Nathan Oxley's place—all night.'

With the back of her hand Rhea rubbed at the water still coursing down her cheeks. 'I wasn't! I was in bed—here, at home—our... no, *your home.*' Then she remembered how determined she had been to get even with him, and had deliberately unplugged the telephone sockets. Which meant he wouldn't believe her, however much she denied spending the night with Nathan.

'S-so what if I was?' she defied him, not caring that she was making matters worse. 'You—you were well occupied too, making love to——' *Too*, she'd said, which would imply, in Leo's eyes, that she, Rhea, had indeed been with Nathan. She looked up at him, sick at heart, frightened by the look in his eyes.

'Ours—ours would be an open marriage, you said,' again realising too late how much she was incriminating herself, how her words still implied that she had a relationship going with Nathan.

She shivered under his icy regard, then the trembling intensified and she realised how cold she was feeling, how wet she was from her precipitate race up and down the village street. 'No ties, no conditions...'

'No woman,' he rasped, his hands gripping her hips, 'no *man* makes a cuckold of me!'

He propelled her backwards into his bedroom and jerked her against him, divesting her forcibly of her jacket. Then his mouth hit hers, drawing from her a cry of protest which, as he worked at her lips until they parted under his forceful persuasion, turned into a groan of despair mixed with helpless surrender.

Her legs grew weak, her arms crept around his neck and her body sagged against his, the intimate contact telling her how aroused he had become. Her lips throbbed under the stimulus of his kisses, trembling as his mouth gentled slightly, firming again as her resistance crumbled entirely away, her thirsting mouth allowing him all the access he demanded.

Conquest of an unwilling woman, that was all it was, she thought, gasping for the air he was denying her. Slowly but surely, she at last conceded, he *was* conquering her, imposing his will and his domination on her.

When at last he let her go, she crumpled at his feet, a wet and shivering human form that must have touched his compassion, if not his warmth, since he lifted her up and appraised her shaking body.

'OK, strip,' he ordered, waiting, hands on hips, for her to obey him. 'For Pete's sake,' as she hesitated, 'I've seen you naked before.' His dark-browed gaze was filled with reminiscence. Impatient at her slow movements, he unfastened her blouse buttons and made short work of the bra beneath it.

Her arms went across her breasts in spite of his mocking smile at her over-modest action. 'Leave the r-rest,' she stammered, but he was deaf to her plea. They followed the other garments, forming a damp pile on the floor.

Plainly the sight of her inflamed him even more, and he swept her pliant body on to the bed and, tugging away his own meager cover, proceeded to make devastating love to her.

'You can't, you mustn't,' she croaked as his lips savoured her throat, her breasts and beyond, 'not now, not at this time of day.'

'To hell with the time of day,' he returned thickly. 'I can make love to you whenever I please—remember that. And I'm going to make sure you remember this. And this. And this.'

She gasped and cried out at the pleasure he was giving her, the intimacy of his kisses, the places he kept discovering that aroused her almost beyond endurance. At last she pleaded with him to take her, but still he kept her waiting. Relenting at last, he possessed her, and this was so complete that she felt she would die in his arms.

A long time later he rolled off the bed, tugging her into his arms and carrying her into the shower. The water cascaded over them, and again he took her into his arms, only the ring of the telephone preventing him from taking her all over again.

It was a business call, and by the time it was finished Rhea had dried herself and run to her own room to find dry clothes.

He came in to find her combing her hair. Narrowed eyes settled on the mirror's image of her face, flushed and radiant from the aftermath of his lovemaking.

'Why were you here, when Uncle Timmy said you'd be at the forge?' she demanded.

'He must have forgotten I've got an appointment with a potential customer—someone who was at the party last night and admired the Dower craftsmanship. He wants something similar for the entrance to his drive.'

'Are you taking Sonya?'

Leo smiled at the sarcastic undertone. 'Maybe, maybe not.'

'All right,' she turned on him fiercely, crying inside because the joy they had just shared, the beautiful act of *love*, had been to him merely an act of *lust*, 'take her. I don't care one way or the other. It's the old sordid story, isn't it?' she added bitterly. 'I can see it in headlines. Boss's ego boosted by adoration of secretary. Takes her everywhere, even to bed.'

His lips thinned, his hands lifted, curling and un-curling. 'I could do this,' he fitted them round her neck, making her shiver, 'or I could up-end you and give you a hiding you'd never forget.'

Bravely her eyes held his and his hands around her neck softened to a caress, turning her legs to water as desire tugged at her insides.

'For your information,' he said on a calmer note, 'Sonya only helps me with the paperwork as a sideline. She happens to be a designer with an established reputation.' He put a couple of paces between them. 'Eat your heart out, Rhea Dower. You're not the only one with artistic ability.'

Jealousy, even stronger than before, fountained inside her. Sonya, the woman who has everything, she thought sourly. 'I never claimed I was,' she snapped. 'It also shows—doesn't it—that Leo Dower likes his women not only to be attractive, but intelligent. Good for you, Mr Dower!'

He smiled at her sarcasm and watched her go to the door. 'Where now?'

'It's stopped raining, so I'll walk. Back to Nathan's.' She steeled herself for his black gaze, which duly came her way. 'To *work*. And, unlike you, I don't mix *pleasure* with it.'

Early evening, Leo telephoned. Nathan, hands thickly coated with clay, asked Rhea to answer it. She was wrist-deep in dye, so she seized a cloth to hold the instrument.

'Thought I'd find you still there,' her husband's voice drawled, 'but why the long delay?'

'In answering? We were—er—otherwise engaged,' she retorted, deliberately provoking him. 'Couldn't you guess?'

Nathan shook his head. 'Don't do that to him,' he whispered, and Rhea coloured deeply.

'If I thought you were speaking the truth,' Leo spat through teeth that were clearly clenched, 'I'd——'

'Why did you call?' Rhea asked, contrite now, but unable to convey it through her voice.

'To tell you I'd be late home.'

'Thanks, but, knowing that Sonya's with you, I'd be surprised if you came home at all,' Rhea returned, angry again.

'We've been invited to stay to dinner.' His tone showed that he too was angry. 'I'll see you in the morning.'

'Will you?' She ended the call quickly, afraid that he might detect the tears in her voice. After the swift and devastating passion of their middle-of-the-day love-making, their cold, ill-humoured conversation left her feeling shattered. She tried to lose herself in her work, but was glad when Carrie called round, inviting them to a meal at her and Vince's guesthouse.

Rhea spent most of the evening talking to Vince, if only to give Carrie the chance of monopolising Nathan, which she clearly wished to do. Rhea could not understand how oblivious Nathan seemed to be of Carrie's liking for him—more than liking, Rhea was sure.

When Vince offered to give her a lift home, she jumped at it, even though Nathan said he would do the honours. Rhea had seen the pleasure in Carrie's eyes as Vince made the announcement, and trusted that the man responsible for its being there might see it too.

Vince drew away with a wave as soon as Rhea opened the cottage door, although he did not see her hesitate before closing it. Leo was there, but he wasn't alone. How, Rhea wondered, could she have been so stupid as to believe he would be?

His cold stare made her want to sink into the ground, but she was darned if she would give him an explanation of her lateness—it was almost midnight—in front of Sonya Selby. Let him think she had been at Nathan's, let him think Nathan had just dropped her at the door. What's more, she thought, I'm darned if I'll play hostess to his girlfriend!

'I'm tired,' she said with a commendable coolness, 'so will you please excuse me?'

'Oh, Rhea—if I may call you that? Must you go? I was so looking forward to a heart-to-heart about our mutual subject.' Sonya gestured to the seat beside her. As if, Rhea fumed, not moving, *she's* the hostess and *I'm* the guest.

Catching the mockery in Leo's gaze, she had to suppress the urge to hit him.

'I adore your skirt, Rhea,' Sonya was saying. 'I can see we share a love of bright colours. Would you—could you make me one like that? Not an exact copy, of course, but something similar?'

Rhea could not decide whether Sonya was really making an effort to be friendly—what wife could ever be, Rhea found herself wondering, with her husband's *mistress*?—or coveted something she knew perfectly well she couldn't have? Or was Sonya subtly telling her, 'I know darned well your skirt is homemade, and what's more, in case you don't know, it looks it.'

'Thanks for the compliment,' Rhea heard herself say, 'but I'm very busy at the moment making things for the craft fair. I'll bear your request in mind, though. Goodnight, Miss Selby.' With a look that mixed defiance with accusation, she added insinuatingly, 'Goodnight, Leo. Enjoy your night's *rest.*'

The days took on a pattern, with Leo leaving early for his work at the forge, and Rhea staying late at Nathan's. Like her, Nathan was working flat out to make enough pottery to fill his stall.

In between completing her own fabric designs and, with Carrie's help, making them up into skirts and tops, wall-hangings and lampshades, Rhea kept her promise to Nathan and fitted in the decoration of his ornaments, his bowls, jugs and flower vases.

Consequently, each evening on returning home, she was completely exhausted, falling asleep as soon as her head burrowed into the pillow. Once, she could have sworn her door had opened and that someone had entered, but on stirring and sleepily opening her eyes, she found that no one was there.

Another time, in the early morning, birdsong awakened her, and she turned on to her back to listen.

Her arm came up against a human form and she almost cried out in terror, until she discovered what had really awakened her—Leo's arm across her breasts, his demanding hands pulling her towards him. He was, she discovered, naked.

'How...' she croaked '...when...?'

'Did I get into your bed? In the early hours. If a man can't sleep, he does the sensible thing—he goes and finds a woman. In this case, *his* woman. Come on, baby,' he commanded, his tongue busy around her ears, making tingling trails around them, 'I'm making love to you right here, right now.' In no time, her nightdress was disposed of over the side of the bed.

'Leo, no...' Already she was shivering in anticipation of his caresses.

'You know damned well it's "Leo, yes,"' he growled, fitting his mouth over hers and stifling any further attempts on her part to dissuade him. She didn't want to, she discovered; she wanted him with all her heart and soul. She turned into him and lost herself in his overpowering masculinity, knowing his needs now and matching them with her own, feeling her insides alternately curl and unfurl, while her body ached for his intrusion, yet loving the torment with which he promised yet withheld the ultimate joy, rejoicing at last in his complete and utter possession of her.

When she awoke for the second time, she discovered that, yet again, she was alone. It was, she thought hazily, like being made love to by a mystery lover, one who came in the dark hours and took her, then disappeared until the next time and the next...

Then she reproached herself for being a romantic fool, because the man in *her* life needed her, wanted her for only one reason, the satisfaction of his male desires. Which was precisely why he had come to her in the night when, he had said, he had not been able to sleep.

Every morning she hoped to see him at breakfast; every evening she tried to stay awake until he returned. She began to believe that she had dreamt they shared the same house, that maybe he didn't exist except in her thoughts and her dreams!

When she saw him again, it was in the pub one lunchtime. For days she had made up her own sandwiches, eating them as she worked. This particular day, she went with Nathan to the Dog and Badger for sandwiches and a drink.

Leo was at the bar, his back to her, but even so her heart thumped and her muscles contracted with excitement, her body starting to ache for him.

He turned and caught her eyes upon him. As if he had guessed her thoughts, he smiled, and her heart turned over, but it soon righted itself as she detected mockery in his eyes.

'Rhea, lass,' Timmy spoke from a dark corner, 'it's a long time since I saw you. Nathan, bring her across. Leo, get your wife a drink, will you?' he shouted. 'And your old friend Nathan too.'

Leo looked with anything but friendly eyes at the man to whom Timmy had referred, but he obliged his uncle and bought drinks all round, bringing them to the circular table and taking the seat beside his wife, Nathan having tactfully joined Timmy on the high-backed wall seat.

'Busy, then, are you?' commented Timmy, noticing Rhea's paint-stained hands. 'Dyeing again?' he joked.

'Partly, yes,' Rhea replied, over-conscious of her husband's interest even though he was drawing deeply on the contents of his beer glass. 'Mostly, it's paint. I'm decorating some of Nathan's pottery.'

'After biscuit firing, or before?' Leo asked casually, separating his sandwiches and chewing one.

She glanced at him with surprise. She had expected hostility because it was Nathan for whom she was working, not informed interest. 'After,' she answered, looking at him fully for the first time since he had joined them. 'Before glazing takes place.'

He returned her gaze, and she was intoxicatingly aware that their ensuing silent exchange had nothing whatever to do with the subject in hand, and everything to do with intimacy and passion and desire.

'Painting with pigments, that is, metal oxides or underglaze colours...' Her voice trailed into silence, while her heartbeats almost deafened her.

'You're talking,' Nathan commented with a smile, 'like someone who's made pots all her life.'

Rhea moistened her lips, which had become strangely dry, dragging her eyes from Leo's. 'It's only what you've taught me about decorating pottery,' she returned. 'It wasn't part of my degree syllabus.'

'You've been a very apt pupil,' Nathan told her, apparently engrossed in estimating the depth of the froth on his beer.

Leo's expression registered irritation-plus, which must have flowed through him to his feet, since he rose abruptly, nodded unsmilingly to his wife and her companion and pushed in his chair with a clatter. 'Coming, Timmy?'

Timmy nodded, making a rueful face at Rhea, and followed his nephew outside. Nathan let out a sigh. Whether it was one of relief, or an expression of bewilderment at the ways of husbands and wives, bearing in mind his own experience in that respect, Rhea could not tell.

A few days before the craft fair was due to open, Rhea found Leo still at home when she came down for breakfast. He wore a suit and tie and an air of business to come in the big city hung around him.

'How long this time?' she asked, putting her sinking heart firmly back in place and anticipating his an-

nouncement of yet another period of absence from
home.

A shrug of broad shoulders was followed by a clipped,
'Who knows?'

'It depends,' she heard herself burst out, 'on the whim
of Miss Selby, no doubt.'

A quizzical I'm-not-telling eyebrow lifted. 'Who
knows?' he repeated with a sardonic smile.

His arm came out and swung her to him, taking her
so much by surprise that she had no time to erect her
barriers. His hands cupped her face and his brilliant gaze
stared into her wide eyes. 'Anyone would think,' he
commented drily, 'that you were jealous.'

She tried to struggle free. 'Not on your life,' she retorted. 'Feel free to *take* any woman you want.'

He laughed at the deliberate double meaning, lowered
his head, helped himself to a long and devastating kiss
and left, picking up his executive case as he went.

The nights were lonely and long, but the work Rhea
had to get through before the fair opened kept her hands
busy in the daytime, and at night her mind preoccupied
in between bouts of restless sleeping.

Two evenings before the opening, she worked without
pause, except for a snatched evening meal of soup and
fruit and coffee.

Nathan mopped his brow. 'Sorry to mention it, Rhea,'
he said, 'but there are half a dozen more jugs ready for
decorating.'

Carrie worked at a sewing-machine in another room,
putting together skirts and tops which Rhea had de-
signed and processed. She joined the others for the sparse
snack, sinking down wearily in the only uncluttered chair
in the room.

'I'm glad my knitted offerings are all pressed and
packaged,' she sighed, 'ready for Vince to take to the
hall. He'll take all these too, Nathan,' indicating his

work, 'not to mention your stuff, Rhea. Tommy said he'd help us with our stalls if we wanted.'

'Nice of him,' commented Nathan offhandedly, 'but he'll be too busy setting up his clocks to worry about us.' He smiled at Carrie. 'I'll be your strong man, love, OK?'

Carrie smiled back, and Rhea rejoiced in the way the two of them seemed to share some wonderful secret. She had, in fact, suspected that Carrie might have stayed more than once at Nathan's overnight and had been glad beyond words.

It did not occur to her then that she also might stay at Nathan's overnight, but that was exactly what she did. It was well into the small hours when she surfaced and the three of them ground to a halt.

'No need to go,' Nathan told her. 'There's a folding bed over there. Use that, Rhea. You're almost falling asleep on your feet—isn't she, Carrie?'

'I've got a spare toothbrush somewhere,' Carrie said, backing Nathan up, and watching as, with a few quick movements, he made a space and unfolded the bed. 'I'll get some bedclothes. It's OK, I know where they are, Nathan, love.' His hand touched hers as she passed him.

Gratefully Rhea accepted all the offers, dropping asleep almost as soon as the light was out. Carrie was there next morning. Rhea schooled herself to show no surprise, but Carrie caught her in the kitchen making the toast.

'Rhea, I have to tell you, or I'll burst!' she confided. 'Nathan said I could. He's asked me to marry him!' She half disappeared into Rhea's delighted hug. 'It won't be for a while, because he wants to clear the business of his divorce out of the way, but he's going to give me a ring. Can I see what your engagement ring's like, to help me decide what I want?'

She looked at Rhea's wedding finger, which bore only a plain gold band. What Carrie didn't know, Rhea reflected, and never would, was that that ring was there as a symbol of vengeance fulfilled.

'Leo didn't give me one, Carrie,' Rhea said simply. He didn't think I was worth the expenditure, she almost said, but kept the bitter words to herself.

'That's OK,' said Carrie brightly and tactfully, 'some couples don't bother these days. I'll just have to look in shop windows, won't I?'

'A bottle of champagne seems to be called for, Nathan,' Rhea commented with a broad smile as Nathan entered, reaching up to kiss his cheek. 'Congrats, both of you. I'm really delighted.'

'Don't tell anyone, will you?' Carrie urged. 'Not yet, not until I tell you you can. Promise?'

'I promise,' Rhea answered solemnly.

The next evening she stayed at Nathan's again. They had worked all day setting up the stalls around the hall in the town. This time Carrie went home. It was, she said, her evening on duty and Vince's night off.

The day of the craft show dawned bright and clear. Carrie called Nathan, then asked to speak to Rhea.

'Don't forget the party after the show tonight,' Carrie reminded her. 'Wearing something nice?'

'One of my own creations,' Rhea pretended to boast. 'How about you?'

'One of my handknits,' she answered with a laugh. 'Nothing like modelling your own designs to encourage people to place orders!'

Saturday crowds thronged the town's streets, and as soon as the doors opened people drifted in.

Timmy sat near the door collecting the entrance money which would go towards the cost of hiring the hall. The remainder, they had all agreed, would be divided between the exhibitors so that even those whose sales were low or non-existent would receive some payment for their efforts.

In a spare moment from the rush of customers, Rhea glanced round the hall to try and judge how the fair was going. Around Maisie Kelney's leatherwork stall three or four people lingered, while Mildred Smith seemed to be doing a fair trade in corn dollies.

To her delight, Carrie's handknits were doing so well that she mopped her brow on catching Rhea's eye. At the stall next to hers, Nathan's customers were exclaiming over his decorated pottery and, it seemed, parting willingly with their money.

Then the customers swooped on Rhea's goods again, which meant that she didn't see a couple enter, one of whom paid the entrance fee for them both. Busy answering queries about her fabric and her designs, she did not hear the woman enquiring the whereabouts of 'Rhea Dower's stall'.

It was not until the crowd had temporarily cleared again that she saw the couple approaching.

'Now, Rhea,' exclaimed Sonya, 'this is a situation where the seller can't refuse a buyer. You forgot my request to you, didn't you,' she went on over-sweetly, 'to make me a skirt like yours? So,' her eyes flitted from one item to the other, 'now I'm going to make my choice. If I buy up all your goods, you won't be able to grumble, will you?'

'Take your pick, Miss Selby,' Rhea commented indifferently. 'Just as long as you don't choose the things people have reserved and paid for.'

'Rhea!' There was rebuke in Leo's tone, while a warning flashed in his eyes.

Colouring with annoyance, she flashed right back, telling him silently, I can dispose how I like of my handiwork. When Sonya chose a skirt with a design similar to the one she had recently admired, Rhea made no demur, waiting as Sonya went on riffling through the fabrics and pulling a particularly dazzling design from the pile.

It was one of Rhea's favourites and she hated the idea of its gracing Sonya's person when made up, but her face was without expression as she accepted Sonya's cheque and wrapped the items, handing them over.

'Hi, Nathan,' said Sonya, moving to the next stall.

'Thanks for letting me know,' Rhea murmured, her wide eyes resting angrily on her husband, 'of your return. With your girlfriend in tow, as usual,' she couldn't stop herself from adding.

His smile was sarcastic and fleeting. 'I tried ringing you. No answer, *as usual.*' He echoed her words tartly.

'I—I——' Rhea just prevented the hot colour from swamping her cheeks. If she told him the truth, that she had spent two nights at Nathan's, he would put an entirely false construction on the statement. Nor could she tell him that Carrie had stayed there for one of those nights. She couldn't tell him either that Carrie and Nathan were deeply in love and were engaged to be married. 'I guess I must have been tired,' she finished weakly, pretending to be absorbed in sorting through the goods on display.

'Be honest and admit that you didn't answer the phone in case I was the caller?'

'Maybe, maybe,' she answered offhandedly as, to her relief, customers drifted round her stall, causing Leo to move on. How else could she have answered? she asked herself helplessly, but she did not miss the touch of scepticism in his eyes.

CHAPTER TEN

THE closing of the doors brought sighs of relief and, for the most part, a deep satisfaction. Sales had been high and everyone had sold something.

'See you back here tonight,' people were calling as they left the hall, stalls dismantled and disposed of, unsold goods boxed and taken home.

Rhea was surprised to find the cottage empty, then told herself to come down to earth and remember that Sonya Selby's charms were, in Leo's eyes, greater than hers. After all, she reflected cynically as she showered and brushed her hair until it crackled, Sonya had been on the the scene—Leo's scene—long before she, Rhea Hirst, had appeared on it.

She was searching for her jacket among the others on the hallstand—her nostrils picking up Leo's musky and warmly familiar scent as she foraged—when the door opened and he came in.

Finding what she was looking for at that moment, Rhea swung round, her expression full of fight, but Leo was alone. He smiled as if he had guessed her thoughts, then looked her over, clearly liking what he saw.

'Colourful and flattering. You should sew a label into your creations,' he commented, 'and set up in business as a fashion designer.'

'Joining forces with your girlfriend, I suppose you're going to add? No, thank you. If you're hungry——'

'I've eaten.'

'With Sonya.'

159

'With my uncle.' His hands on her hips eased her towards him. 'I do believe——' His mouth approached hers, but she struggled free.

'I am not jealous!' The words came out slowly and emphatically. But you are, a tiny voice whispered, you most certainly are...

'I don't know what time I'll be home,' she threw over her shoulder as she pulled on her jacket, then dashed out before he could insist on giving her a lift.

She was dancing with Nathan when Leo appeared in the doorway. She faltered and Nathan steadied her, asking, 'You OK?'

She nodded and concentrated on the lively steps, telling herself to pretend that Leo wasn't there, telling her heart to stop pounding so much harder just because the man she loved but who did not love her had arrived on the scene.

Dance over, she smiled at Nathan, who returned the smile briefly before allowing his eyes to wander in search of Carrie.

'She's over there,' Rhea nodded across the room, 'with Mildred and Maisie. Want to go to her?'

Reluctantly he shook his head. 'If Carrie and I are seen together too much people will start to talk, and we don't want that. Not yet, not until the legalities of my affairs have been settled. You do understand, Rhea?'

'Of course I do.'

The music started again, and Nathan's hand was coming out to take hers when another hand forestalled him, one that was stronger, more forceful, and had every right to be, in the circumstances. A hand that hammered and shaped incandescent metal, arms that wielded heavy tools, risking injury and heat-burns, pitting his strength and his will-power against even more powerful forces.

The arms she was swept into held a promise of shared delight which over the weeks had become practically irresistible. By an irony of fate, the weapon with which she had chosen to wreak vengeance on the Dowers had been turned on to her, and the hurt it was inflicting was almost too painful to endure.

Fingers tilted her face. 'Solemn thoughts, or annoyance that I took you away from Oxley?'

In spite of herself, Rhea smiled. 'Possibly to the first, definitely no to the second.'

'So tell me those thoughts.'

This time her smile defied him. 'Not on your life!'

'I could make you.' His eyes were full of meaning, hinting at past intimacies and those to come. He seemed amused at her discomfiture.

'Maybe you could,' she concurred, head on one side, 'but it wouldn't have any meaning. It would be just a means of satisfying your...our...passing...um...sensual needs, not to mention a way of demonstrating your physical domination over me. Our marriage was never meant to contain any adhesive element. Nor,' she moistened her lips which had become curiously dry under his appraisal, 'was there meant to be any intertwining of our emotions.'

'True.' His glance was hooded. 'That was quite a speech. My wife is certainly articulate.'

'I'm *not* your wife,' she returned tartly, irritated because he had tacitly agreed with all her statements.

'So what are you?' He seemed amused. 'My woman?'

'No. Sonya's that,' she riposted angrily, because he didn't dispute her allegation either by word or shake of the head.

He held her closer, forcing her to dance more intimately with him. Her head went back and she could not prevent her eyes entangling with his, her fingers digging into the casual shirt he wore, her thighs touching his, encased in denim.

Amused, he flicked the long leather 'fun' earrings she had bought from Mildred Smith's stall, touched the matching choker with fingers that lingered, making the nerves of her skin dance at the cool, very personal contact.

'How did the craft fair go?' he asked as their bodies moved in perfect harmony.

'For me, very well. I've got a pile of orders, weeks of work ahead. One day,' she grew dreamy, 'I'd like to start a business of my own.' That would be when her marriage to him came to an end. Her eyes closed on the thought so that he wouldn't see in them the deep distress the thought engendered within her.

'Rhea.' He had whispered her name and her eyes fluttered open, her head tilting back.

As if her lips held a magnet his mouth came down, and hers willingly succumbed to his possession. His kiss made her senses swim, an exquisite ache throb deep inside her. The kiss had no end, and its effect on her was such that it was as though she had drunk too much intoxicating liquid, except that she hadn't touched a drop.

A buzz of conversation at the door turned into a mild commotion, and Leo broke the kiss, turning his head, his hold slackening. Heart sinking, Rhea guessed the identity of the new arrival.

For the rest of the dance, Leo's mind was plainly elsewhere, his movements becoming automatic. She broke away from him, the other dancers moving round them.

'What prompted that?' he queried, frowning.

'How can you pretend you don't know?' she retorted. 'Your girlfriend's on a telepathic line to you. Why don't you pick up your mental phone and answer her?'

She had meant the sarcasm to jolt him so that he returned to her in mind as well as body, but, to her dismay and disappointment, he took her statement literally.

'I'll take you at your word,' he clipped. 'If you'll excuse me...'

'You're not going to leave me standing here?' Rhea wailed.

An eyebrow flicked, a mocking smile flirted with his lips. 'You don't like being stood up? OK, so come with me and you'll be able to hear what we have to say to each other.' He took her hand to pull her behind him, but she snatched it free. 'It's business, pure and simple.'

'Go to her,' she choked, not believing him. 'Go to the woman you really want!' She spied Nathan alone on the edge of the circulating couples and made a beeline. 'Dance with me, Nathan,' she pleaded through quivering lips, and urged him on to the dance-floor.

Leo's contemptuous glance over the heads of the crowd made her shiver inside, but she moved with Nathan as if there were no greater pleasure than to be dancing with him. Deliberately she turned her back to her husband, but swinging round in the course of the dance, she saw him moving slowly round the floor with Sonya. He was listening intently to her words, his head inclined slightly the better to hear her. And the better, no doubt, Rhea thought angrily, to inhale her perfume and feel her warm breath on his cheek.

'Domestic quarrel?' Nathan asked with an understanding smile.

'Sort of. Take me home, Nathan,' she said, suppressing the tears that would spring, in spite of herself. 'Don't ask why.'

A glance around was sufficient for Nathan to guess the reason, and he cheerfully obeyed, first signalling to Carrie, who nodded, understanding at once.

'Thanks,' said Rhea as he drew up in the parking space at the rear of River Cottage. 'And thanks, Nathan, for helping me. I mean, for letting me invade your studio all this time, not to mention letting me stay a couple of nights. You're very good, you know, and Carrie's lucky.' She leaned across and pecked him on the cheek.

He smiled in the semi-darkness of the car. 'Am I allowed to return the compliment?' He kissed her too, on the cheek. 'Leo's a lucky man.'

She shook her head fiercely. 'He's not, Nathan. If only you knew the true situation!'

'Tell me some time.'

'Maybe. Goodnight.' She waved as he drove away.

Searching for her key, she used a small pocket torch to pick her way to the front door. As she reached it, a man came from out of the shadows behind her, and she screamed, a hand to her throat.

He took her torch from her trembling hand and flashed it upward at his own face. Stark terror was only fractionally modified by relief and recognition.

'Oh, God,' she croaked, 'did you have to behave like a would-be criminal and give me such a terrible fright?'

'A *would-be* criminal?' Jerome remarked lightly. 'I thought that, in your eyes, I was the devil in disguise where lawbreaking was concerned.'

Even when they faced each other across the living-room, Rhea could not stop herself trembling. She sank into a chair.

'You need a drink, Mrs Dower,' Jerome declared, moving towards the sideboard. 'No, don't get up.' She had made no move to do so. 'I know where the goodies are. I lived here once. What's yours? Nothing?' He helped himself, lifting the glass in an ironic toast. 'So how's my big brother treating you?' He looked her up and down. 'Can't you stop shaking? Why not? Got a guilty conscience?'

That was too much to take. '*Guilty conscience*?' she exploded, anger quelling the remaining symptoms of fright. 'For heaven's sake, you were the guilty one, Jerome, not me!'

A car drew up, scrunching to a stop. Waiting, Jerome stared apprehensively at the door.

Leo thrust into the cottage. 'What the hell did you mean, Rhea, by leaving without telling me?' Then he saw Jerome and froze. 'Good God! The embezzler returns!'

Jerome made a face, taking a drink. 'So she's told you, then?' he commented guardedly. 'How much, Rhea?'

'Enough,' was her equally guarded answer.

'You admit it?' his brother asked briskly.

'Admit what? I admit nothing. That's what my lawyer told me to say, at all times. Even to my own *dear* brother.' He raised his glass. 'To old times, Leo.' He drank.

It was, Rhea sensed, Jerome's way of reminding his brother of the days long ago that Timmy had told her about, when Leo had protected Jerome after their mother had died. And, from Leo's expression, Rhea saw that he knew it too, but whether Jerome had touched his sympathy as well as his memory she could not tell.

Looking from one to the other, she wondered how she had ever thought they were alike. Maybe they were physically, except that there was a weakness about Jerome's eyes and mouth, whereas there was strength of character and purpose in every angle and plane of Leo's face, a face she loved to touch, to kiss, a face she *loved*.

Jerome took a seat as though he belonged, which he probably did, Rhea conceded reluctantly, certainly more than she. Then he moved, putting himself beside her on the sofa. She jerked away, and he laughed unkindly.

'Still a cold fish, Rhea?' he taunted, draining his glass and disposing of it. 'Hasn't even Leo's virile heat thawed you out?' He turned to his brother. 'She went all iceberg on me, Leo, even though she wore my ring, so of course I held my horses, as they say.'

He spoke as if he had rehearsed every word, like a defendant in court who had learned his lawyer's briefing by heart.

'It's not my line to take a woman cold,' he blustered on. 'Nor did I want her running to her precious father, yelling, "He's raped me, fire him, Daddy." I thought of all that lovely money I'd forfeit by forcing myself on her. Anyway,' he looked with amusement on Rhea's aghast gaze, 'I stood her *coyness* stoically because I knew there were plenty of other women I could have fun with, without recriminations, or losing my very well-paid job, and I did.'

'Why, you——!' Unable to contain her fury, Rhea sprang at him, grasping his tie, tugging at his hair, pulling with all her might, despite his shouts for mercy.

'You rotten low-down louse!' she accused, sobbing and struggling as Leo gripped her shoulders, forcing her away and to her feet. She fought him too, until he captured her hands and grasped them behind her back.

She turned blazing eyes on him. 'I hate your brother, I hate you! I hate the Dowers, except Uncle Timmy. I don't know how I even brought myself to marry you, Leo Dower.' You *do,* a treacherous voice prompted. You loved him, that's why. You still do...

'Hey, has she got fire!' Jerome commented, his gaze frankly admiring. 'And I never knew. How does she measure up in——?'

'Don't you dare,' she cried hoarsely at Leo, desperate to free herself, 'don't you dare answer that question! If you do, I'll——' In vain, she struggled, but Leo held her easily, stilling her violent efforts until the pain of his restraining hands became unbearable. She lifted tear-stained eyes to his. 'Please, Leo, you're hurting!'

He released her at once, his face a mask.

'I'll tell you something, Jerome,' he said as she sank down in a chair, away from them both, but Leo approached her and she shrank away. He lifted her hand and indicated her wedding finger. 'This is her ring of revenge. She married me, letting me believe she was pregnant by you——'

'I told you the truth,' she broke in, 'that I wasn't——'

'She married me,' Leo went on implacably, 'to have her own back on you, on me, on the Dowers.' He moved away from her. 'She doesn't love me, but what she does love is what I give her——'

'So to speak,' Jerome interposed with a snigger, but his brother went on,

'The way my bank balance enables her to live in the way to which she was accustomed before you robbed her, or so she alleges.'

Rhea's head shot up. 'There it is again,' she accused, 'your brotherly instinct from the past to protect your little brother! *Alleged*, you said. There's so much evidence to prove he defrauded Daniel Hirst that it would fill a volume.'

Jerome began to look perturbed. Was he feeling, Rhea wondered, that the net was closing on him? His expression brightened as if he had thought of a way out.

'There are one or two things you should know about your beautiful wife, Leo, and, as your brother, I think I should warn you.'

Leo's cold eyes swung to Rhea, then back to Jerome. 'Well?'

'If you slander me,' Rhea warned grimly, 'I'll sue.'

'Where are the witnesses?' Jerome gibed. 'My sibling wouldn't testify against me. We were too close as boys.' He walked about like a lawyer in a courtroom. 'I had a drink in the Dog and Badger while I was waiting for you both to come back.'

He paused for effect, and Rhea's heart began to pound as a strange foreboding gripped her.

'The rumour's going round,' Jerome swaggered up to Rhea and away again, 'that while this lady's husband was away she slept for a couple of nights with Nathan Oxley.'

'It's not true!' Rhea cried. 'I——'

'You swear,' Leo approached, his face dark with anger, 'that this rumour's not true? You spent every night here in this cottage?'

'N-no, not every...' What was the use, she thought, of prevaricating? 'So what if I did stay at Nathan's place?'

'Which was the *real* reason why my phone calls stayed unanswered,' he gritted.

'There you are,' said Jerome triumphantly.

'Will you be quiet?' Rhea cried furiously. 'We were working flat out, Leo, to get finished before the show. I worked one night until the early hours. Nathan invited me to stay——'

'In his bed?' Leo rasped.

'No! Carrie was there too.' It could have been her trump card had she been permitted to play it, but her promise to her friends not to reveal their engagement bound her to silence.

'Sharing your room?'

'No.' I used the studio... The words tormented her tongue, but she could not speak them without letting Nathan and Carrie down.

'There you are!' exclaimed Jerome, eyes shining with triumph, and not a little spite. 'What's more,' he confronted her, hands behind his back, still playing the prosecuting lawyer, 'are you going to deny, Rhea, that when Nathan brought you home this evening you kissed him? And that he kissed you?'

'It wasn't a kiss,' she corrected, whispering now, 'it was just a peck I gave him, which he returned. I was thanking him for——'

'An entertaining couple of nights?' Leo snarled.

'For God's sake,' she shrieked, hands covering her ears, 'it's like being savaged by two vicious dogs!'

Jerome smiled unpleasantly, walking away. 'I rest my case.'

There was a long silence while Rhea sat back, eyes closed, face pale.

'You robbed her, Jerome,' Leo pronounced at last. 'You'll repay her—every penny, every cent. Do you hear?'

Jerome paled, dropping into a chair. 'I can't.'

Leo swung to him. 'You mean it's all too securely tied up?'

'No.'

'You've surely got it invested somewhere?'

'Nope.' Jerome sat forward, staring at his clasped hands. 'I spent it all, Leo, honestly. That's why I came here.' He shifted uncomfortably. 'Cash-flow problems, so to speak.'

Older brother turned on younger. 'Get out!' Rhea had never seen Leo look so angry.

'Where to, Leo?' Jerome whined. 'I thought you could put up me here for a couple of nights.' Leo's answering stare was so vitriolic that Jerome winced. He got up slowly, shoving his hands into his jacket pockets. 'Uncle Timmy won't turn me out. He's got a heart, unlike you. So long, Rhea, Leo.'

'Before he goes,' Rhea stood, facing them both, 'I want to tell you something else, Leo. Something that only Jerome and I know.'

'Rhea, for God's sake...' Jerome's voice tailed away at the determination in her eyes.

'Leo, your brother was responsible for my parents' deaths. It was his fault their plane crashed.'

'Do you deny this, Jerome?' Leo queried sharply.

Jerome shrugged, then shook his head, staring at the carpet.

'When my father flew the plane back from Scotland— the last time but one that he was to pilot it—he told Jerome he was sure a fault was developing in an engine. It was making a strange noise. Jerome promised faithfully, at my father's request, to have it looked at and overhauled.'

'And he didn't?' Leo asked roughly.

'He didn't. He forgot, he said.'

'My God!' came hoarsely from Leo. 'Get out, Jerome,' he said at last with a dismissing movement of his head.

Jerome's feet dragged across to the door, his hand extending to pick up his travel bag. As the door slammed behind him, Leo asked harshly, 'How sweet is revenge, Rhea? Is it as cloying as syrup? Or does it taste as delectable as honey?'

'Ask yourself, Leo,' she said thickly. 'You also vowed revenge on me—for using you, as you put it. You'd make me pay, you said.' Her eyes lifted heavily to his. 'You've made me pay, Leo, dearly. Are *you* pleased? Are *you* happy now?'

He came to her that night. Unable to sleep, she stood at the window, a wrap loosely around her. She heard the door click shut behind him and all of her senses linked like forged chains to hold her responses back from leaping with expectancy and delight.

'I want you, Rhea,' he said. 'For the last time, you're going to act as my wife. Then——'

She twisted round. He stood there, arms folded, a towelling robe hanging loose, and nothing beneath it.

Desire flooded through her, threatening to swamp her, to stop her escaping. 'You can't, not deliberately, not in cold blood. I won't let you!' She tried to push past him, but he caught her, swung her round and against him.

As her body hit his, dismay fought a running battle with delight. She should be fighting him, dredging up her hatred for the Dower brothers, resisting with all her might the sensual onslaught of this man.

Reason lost out. The familiarity of his body, the musky scent of him that drew her like a magnet, overcame reason and conscious thought, allowing emotion to take control. Her love for him, for everything about him, was almost her undoing, and her resistance almost crumpled. But again her rational self fought back. She couldn't, she wouldn't let him take her knowing how much he hated her, wanting her only to complete the circle of *his* revenge, to prove once more his total domination over her.

'Stop!' she cried. 'How could you do this to me?'

He answered in deeds, not words, disrobing her in a few fluid movements. He swung her to the bed and stood over her supine figure, looking, arms folded, while her toes curled and her pulses hammered at the slow, sensual way he was regarding every part of her.

Desire for him, for his total possession, welled up uncontrollably, making her legs restless and her breaths come faster. He laughed, knowing just what he was doing to her, and the taunting sound of his laughter made her shiver with apprehension, yet *frissons* of excitement coursed through her.

He came to her then, covering her with his body, and she moaned with the pleasure of the intimate contact. He proceeded to make love to her with such controlled voluptuousness, yet such finesse, bringing her such agony and such ecstasy that all she wanted was to become one with him and never, ever, to leave him.

At last he relented, taking her with such complete possession yet holding back the ultimate pleasure for so long that she heard herself gasping his name over and over again, pleading with him to make her finally and irrevocably his.

His arms were round her when she fell asleep, her head against his chest, his legs intertwined with hers, his body her security, her sanctuary.

Waking next morning, she found herself alone. Leo must have disentangled himself from her in the night and walked away from her distastefully clinging arms.

She could tell him now how bitter was the taste of revenge. But how sweet it must have been for *him*.

He had certainly had *his* revenge. He had made her pay for using him, and pay dearly, because she had discovered to her cost that it was no longer possible to hate him, nor even to fool herself into believing she did. Through his ruthless yet passionate lovemaking, his relentless assault on her senses, her body, her emotions, he had made absolutely sure that she would love him and remember him beyond all others, for the rest of her life.

CHAPTER ELEVEN

IN THE cool light of morning, Rhea came down to earth, and the impact was shattering.

She could not stay there any longer, that was abundantly clear. She would go down and confront Leo, demand that he released her, and admit that their marriage, if it had ever been possible to call it that, was at an end.

There was no sign of him. His bed was undisturbed, and this to Rhea could mean only one thing. When he had left her bed, he had gone to the arms of Sonya Selby. There was no denying that *he* had given *her* pleasure and fulfilment, she reflected miserably, but her responses to him had plainly left much to be desired.

She rang Carrie, who answered her query like a woman somewhat distracted. 'A room, Rhea? For you? Oh, dear,' she wailed, 'we're full to bulging. I've even had to get out of my own room to accommodate a guest. All I can suggest is that you contact Nathan. He wouldn't mind at all letting you sleep on the folding bed in his studio. But, Rhea,' as if the strangeness of her friend's request had just struck her, 'for heaven's sake, why? No, forget that, I shouldn't have asked. Maybe in a couple of days we can have you here, but at the moment we're up to our eyes.'

Ask Nathan? Rhea thought, hesitating. Why ever not? she asked herself. Leo wouldn't mind. What had he said last night? 'For the last time, you're going to act as my wife.' Which meant that he had crossed her off his list of acquaintances.

'Use the folding bed again?' Nathan responded, sounding puzzled. 'Of course, but why...? No, forget that. When?'

'Is today OK? Just until Carrie and Vince have a room to spare. I'll be round as soon as I can collect my belongings. And thanks, Nathan, thanks a lot.'

As she was leaving, the telephone rang. She made to answer, held back, then lifted the mouthpiece, listening silently. If it was Leo, she would ring off.

'Leo, is that you?'

'Uncle Timmy,' Rhea answered, 'Leo isn't here.'

'Well, he's not here either, lass. I'm at the forge. He's always here before me, but not today. Know where he's gone, Rhea?'

'I—I was hoping you'd tell me that, Uncle Timmy. I've an idea where he might be found, but——'

'Hm.' Timmy sounded grim. 'Some men don't know when they're lucky.' Which could only confirm, Rhea thought unhappily, that her guess of where—to whom— Leo had gone had been correct. 'When he does come home,' Timmy went on, 'tell him Jerome's left my place. He wouldn't say where he was going either. They're a rum couple, those two brothers,' he finished scratchily. 'Tell him I need him to help me on this job, will you?'

Rhea assured him that she would, but felt bound to add that she didn't know when she would be seeing Leo again. She ended the call quickly, in case Timmy asked her to explain what she meant.

She stayed with Nathan for three nights, not one, sharing his kitchen and his bathroom, and doing her best to lose herself in her work. She had so many orders to fulfil that she knew she would have to work long and hard to get through them.

Even when Carrie and Vince offered her a room for as long as she liked, and into which she gladly moved, Rhea accompanied Nathan each day to the Dog and Badger. They made no attempt to keep it a secret that she had slept at Nathan's again, and worked in his house every day.

There had been no word from Leo. It seemed that he had returned to the forge and helped his uncle finish the project they had been working on together. Then he had gone, leaving Cuttingbeck with no word to his uncle, and certainly not to his wife, as to where he could be found should the need arise.

Rhea worked herself to a standstill, refusing to give in to the intense unhappiness that gripped her. If only, she brooded constantly, she were able to pick up her bags and walk away as easily as she had entered the village, and Leo Dower's life. But with so much work to do, so many people eagerly awaiting her products, she could not bring herself to let them down. Which meant she was tied to the place until the last order had been fulfilled.

Besides, she was beginning to suspect that something was happening to her, something that she must at all costs keep to herself. Then her suspicions were confirmed and the restraint she had imposed on her emotions, her feelings for Leo, broke down. When she confided her news to Carrie, who was chatting to her one evening in her room, she burst into tears and sobbed her heart out.

The irony of the situation was almost too much to bear. Leo had married her to protect, as he thought, his brother's child, and now she really was expecting a baby, who was indubitably his, he was—and there was no doubt in Rhea's mind—in the process of preparing to divorce her.

'Tell him,' Carrie urged, 'tell Leo about the baby.'

'And have him stay married to me out of pity? Never,' Rhea asserted, wiping her eyes. She had to tell Carrie...
'He thinks I'm having an affair with Nathan.'

Carrie looked horrified. 'You're n—— I mean . . . Oh, Rhea, are you?'

'How could you think that of me?' Rhea protested. 'You of all people!' Carrie said over and over again that she was sorry she'd ever asked the question. 'Of course I like Nathan. He's a good man, and I know you'll be very happy.'

'Tell Leo,' Carrie urged, 'tell him about Nathan and me.'

'But you want to keep it a secret, you said. Anyway, it wouldn't do any good. Shall I tell you the real reason Leo married me?' Rhea explained the situation that led up to Leo's proposal. 'So you see, our marriage was only ever meant to be a temporary affair. It had to end some time.'

'But with a baby coming?' Carrie exclaimed.

'If I tell him, I'll be stopping him from getting together again—that is, if he ever parted from her—with the woman he really wants in his life, Sonya Selby.'

At the Dog and Badger next day, Nathan gave the order at the bar counter while Rhea looked around for a seat. Timmy, tucked away into a corner, waved to her, and she joined him.

'How are you, lass?' he asked. 'Where have you been keeping yourself? Leo's in London. I've got a letter from him for you—it came this morning. Here.'

With a shaking hand, Rhea opened the envelope as Timmy added, 'He's attending a conference—Dower Corporation. He's the chief executive, took over from his father. But I told you, didn't I?'

Rhea nodded, then read the letter. 'Dear Rhea,' it ran, 'there are matters I wish to discuss with you. Is it possible for you to come to my hotel,' he gave the address, 'on Monday next?' The date and time were stated. 'If you cannot make this appointment, please inform my secretary at Dower Corporation's head office. Timmy will give you the address. Yours, Leo.'

Her hands, with the letter, fell to her lap. The impersonal tone, the legal proceedings to come—in other words, the first steps towards a divorce, implicit in its formal language, had knocked her sideways.

Nathan stood waiting at the bar, chatting to a friend.

'You look so pale, Rhea,' Timmy remarked worriedly, squeezing her arm. 'What's Leo said that's upset you so?'

Rhea shook her head. 'He just wants to see me, that's all. At the hotel he's staying at in London.' *That's all?* she thought. That's it, more likely, the end of something that had no real beginning.

'Will you go?' She nodded. 'Tell me, lass—don't answer if you don't want to. Do you love him?'

She had to tell this kindly man the truth. 'Uncle Timmy, I'm . . . there's going to be——'

'A *babby*?' His eyes lit up, his hand covered hers on the table. 'I can't tell you how . . . I was so sad when you told me before that there wasn't going to be any child.'

'Promise you won't tell Leo,' she pleaded urgently.

'But he must be told, lass.'

'No, no! He'd insist on our marriage going on, and it can't, not now. He doesn't trust me. He might even say it wasn't——'

'His? But it is,' Timmy broke in. 'You wouldn't be unfaithful to any man, lass. I'm years older than him and I can tell, I can judge a woman's character.'

'Thanks for believing in me, Uncle Timmy. But there's someone else in Leo's life, if not mine.'

'You don't mean Sonya? No, no, lass. He'd never . . .' But Timmy's voice tailed off uncertainly.

'Hi, Timmy,' Nathan said, setting down the drinks and the food. 'Sorry for the delay, Rhea, but they're very busy today. How are things going, Timmy? I hear Leo's gone back to London. I guess he'll return to Cuttingbeck. Can't keep away long from the forge, can he? That young man you've got to help you, is he OK?'

'Coming on nicely, Nathan,' Timmy answered. 'Shows a lot of promise.' To Rhea's relief, the conversation changed course, and she was able to re-read Leo's letter.

It was strange being back in the metropolis. The noise level hit her first, then the milling crowds, the straight, tense faces. The moors, the streams, she realised, the friendly people she had left behind had become so much part of her that, in these packed and uninterested streets, she felt lost.

The taxi dropped her at the hotel and she entered through automatic doors, hoping Leo would be there to greet her. There was no sign of him, and she wandered a little aimlessly around the foyer, pausing by the fountain, watching the spray. She was taken right back to River Cottage and the stream which wound its way past it. A voice that was so familiar it tied her thoughts into knots brought her swiftly back to her surroundings, her heart thumping loudly enough to deafen her.

Leo stood, tall and commanding, the focal point of a semi-circle of attentive people. They hung on his every word, nodding now and then, laughing as he made a final joke, dismissing them.

The man from whom they deferentially took their leave was not the man Rhea had grown to know and love. This man, immaculately dressed, his manner smoothly courteous, was a stranger. Only his hair had defied the grooming procedure the rest of him had consented to, and his eyes too... his eyes which swung towards her as if pulled by some invisible magnet.

He took in her suit, navy blue with a touch of scarlet and a blouse to match. The formal outfit had been intentional. Hadn't he phrased his letter as if this meeting were to be an interview?

As he moved, long-limbed and aloof, towards her, she was for a few seconds denied the ability to breathe. Those eyes, steely grey and piercing, that she had first seen in the semi-darkness of the forge, played over her, tearing her apart.

She wished she had never come, never left the vast silence of the moors, the village that had become part of her.

'I'm glad you made it.' His hand came out—he was actually going to shake her hand as if she were a passing acquaintance? His hand felt cool and firm, with decision and no nonsense in its brief pressure. And not a hint of warmth or friendship, let alone love.

At least, she tried to console herself, it was a way of touching him, the only way from now on in which any form of physical contact could be made. Divorce meant just that, a breaking of every bond that tied them to each other.

No, she thought, looking into his implacable face, that wasn't true, because she had something of him inside her that she could keep for ever—his child.

'I've booked a table,' he was saying. 'Will you have a drink while we make a selection from the menu?'

A drink in the circumstances was what she needed, but how could she tell him the reason for her request for fruit juice?

'Nothing alcoholic?' Eyebrows high, he shrugged.

A waiter took their order, then Leo gave her his attention.

'How's Cuttingbeck?' he asked, tracing with his finger the reflections on the glass table-top. Could he, in his mind's eye, see the village there? Empty, she wanted to answer, without you. Lonely at night, even the river seems tearful as it flows through the darkness.

'Fine,' she answered aloud.

'And your work?'

'Thriving.' Did she have to sound so falsely cheerful? 'Your uncle Timmy—yes, he's fine too, but he's—I think he's missing you.' Oh, God, she thought, how long could she keep up the pretence of cheerfulness?

'I can't see why. He's got an apprentice working for him.'

'He's your uncle, for heaven's sake! There is such a thing as family affection.' Those eyebrows rose again and the irritation in her voice took even Rhea by surprise. It was the result, she knew, of keeping such a tight rein on her emotions.

At Leo's elbow a waiter cleared his throat. 'Your table is ready, sir, madam.'

As the meal progressed, the small talk dried up. Over coffee in the lounge, he leaned back against the sofa they shared, away from her.

'Before we——' He seemed to feel the need to drain his cup, putting it down. 'Before we can get on with living our separate lives,' he resumed, 'there are matters we must discuss.'

Rhea nodded, even though she felt her insides were being put through a shredding machine.

'You told me not so long ago,' he remarked, 'that the one thing you would like to do was to start your own business.'

'I did, but, even though I said it, I knew it would be impossible. I'd need capital, which I haven't got——'

'I'd provide that capital.'

'You? Oh, you mean as a kind of settlement after the divorce?' Her voice sounded brittle even to her own ears. She had to think quickly. Any money that came her way she would need for the baby's welfare. 'Thanks,' was her cautious answer, 'but I——'

'It's money you can't turn down. I've had some research carried out, with Jerome's reluctant help, into the amount of cash he took from your father's firm, therefore from your inheritance. I intend paying that money back to you. The car he stole from you is luckily still intact and well preserved. That also will be returned to you for you to use however you wish. If it were to be sold, the cash could be added to the lump sum I intend paying you.'

Rhea was shaking her head. 'I couldn't take it from you, Leo. I'd written that money off long ago.'

He sat forward, his hands clasped. 'Will you stop acting the hypocrite?' he grated. 'From the beginning I've been aware that you married me only for what I could give you. OK, so Jerome's non-existent child was not the reason, which by elimination left only one thing, your eyes on my bank account. Now our marriage has, as they say, come to the end of its useful life, you collect. I'm freed from an unproductive relationship——'

Unproductive? Rhea thought. I'd laugh hysterically if I weren't on the brink of tears.

'And you'll be free to pursue your affair with Nathan Oxley to whatever end you had in mind.'

'Also,' she had to say it, 'you'll be able to marry Sonya Selby.'

'I have no wish to marry Sonya Selby.'

'And *I* don't want to marry Nathan Oxley!'

Eyebrows raised, Leo smiled without amusement. 'Quits. Snap. Tell me, Rhea, because I'm curious about it. Why not? No, I know the answer already. He's a struggling potter, living hand to mouth. He doesn't earn enough to keep you as I've been able to keep you.'

She had heard that pre-divorce discussions were usually acrimonious, but surely none had been as bitter as this!

She jumped to her feet. 'Thank you for the meal, but you can keep your money. I wouldn't touch a penny, a *cent* of the Dower brothers' money!'

Her footsteps took her towards the swing doors. Leo's arm linked with hers like newly forged chains and he swung her round. 'Come to my room.'

'Not on your——'

Grimly he walked her towards the door which led to the hotel's residential wing. Other guests turned idly, hoping for a scene to brighten their day. Rhea calmed her anger until Leo's key turned and she was in his room, facing him.

'I want to get one thing clear,' she declared, giving rein now to her anger. 'I did not, *did not*——'

'Calm down!' Taking her by surprise, he peeled off her jacket, throwing it aside. 'I intend this to be a civilised conversation.' He walked away, and she made for the door, but he was there before her, turning and pocketing the key.

He removed his own jacket and pushed his hands into his trouser pockets. 'Our marriage was never meant to last. Agreed?'

No, no, she wanted to shout, I don't agree. Cold reason kept her silent. This aloof, distant-eyed man was a total stranger and she wanted to shake him to bring back the man she had known, wielding a hammer, forming a red-hot piece of metal into the shape he desired.

'Agreed,' she answered levelly.

'Right. I'm ready now to free you, so that you can go your own way, marry the man you really want——'

'What man? Can't you understand?' she cried. 'There's no chance that I'll marry Nathan. Ever.' Should she tell? She had been given permission. 'He's engaged to be married—to Caroline Adley. When his own affairs have been straightened out, they'll marry.'

It was as if Leo had been turned to stone.

'Are you telling me that being married to me has caused you to lose Nathan Oxley?'

'*Lose* him? How could I, when I never *had* him? All right, so I slept at his place. That rumour, as repeated in your presence by Jerome, was right in that respect. But where it went wrong was in deducing that I slept *with* Nathan. I didn't, but Carrie did. As a result of which, they became engaged.'

'So?'

'OK, so I'll confess the rest. Then perhaps you'll let me go.' Rhea took a breath. After this, it really would be the end of everything between them. 'You may or may not appreciate that I couldn't face staying at River Cottage after you'd gone, so I tried to reserve a room at Carrie and Vincent Adley's. They were fully booked at that time, so I slept at Nathan's place for two or three nights.'

Leo looked as grim as she thought he might. Bravely she went on,

'Then I moved into Adley Guesthouse. Which brings my confessions up to date. What about you, Leo?' She looked about her. It was a better than average hotel room, well appointed and comfortable. 'When's Sonya coming to join you? Or perhaps you've told her to go shopping until you've settled matters with me——'

Like lightning he moved, and his hand over her mouth did two things—it stopped her talking and started her body throbbing in the old familiar aching way. She *had* to break free, otherwise she would break down, but he plainly had no intention of letting her go.

His hands were on her shoulders now, biting through the blouse. 'Tell me something. When I made love to you, which man were you fantasising that I was—Jerome or Oxley?'

It was too much! Rhea tore away, reaching for her jacket, pulling it on, with shaking hands smoothing her hair. 'Will you start divorce proceedings, please?' she managed in tolerably even tones.

'Oh, no. I leave that *privilege* to you.'

'But I w-wouldn't know h-how to.'

'Easy. Appoint yourself a lawyer. He'll do the rest.'

They faced each other, his eyes coated with frost, hers brimming with tears. 'Before I go,' she said hoarsely, 'I have to thank you for—for everything. Taking me in, giving me a roof while my injured foot healed. For giving me the shelter of your name when you thought I— thought I——'

She couldn't go on, because now she was, *she was*. The tears spilled over. She searched madly for a handkerchief in the depths of her bag and scrubbed her face.

'I d-didn't finish my confession,' she admitted chokily. 'Since we met, there's never been any other man besides—besides——'

'Who? Besides who?' Leo's eyes blazed into hers. 'Tell me, *tell me*!'

She simply had to, if she didn't want to be shaken to pieces. 'You,' she whispered. 'No one else but you.'

There was a smothered exclamation, and the powerful embrace that engulfed her felt so familiar and wonderful that she wanted to cry and laugh at the same time. The heart that she felt had been torn from her when those loving arms had turned cold and ceased to hold her had been restored to her body.

'Get this into that beautiful head of yours, Mrs Dower,' Leo decreed autocratically. 'There's not going to be a divorce, not you from me, nor I from you. Do—you—understand?' Then she was drawn into a kiss that interfered shockingly with her breathing processes, and went on and on until she gasped for mercy.

None was shown, but she didn't mind at all. Nor did she protest when she was lifted to the bed and a body that she loved beyond words joined her there.

'Oh, Leo, darling,' she whispered, 'please be careful.'

'Why?' he murmured, concentrating on caressing with his lips and tongue the burgeoning breasts that he had uncovered by unfastening her blouse.

'We—we mustn't,' she gasped, stroking the back of his head feverishly, 'hurt the baby.'

He lifted his head, eyes alight with astonishment and wonder. 'Repeat that, Rhea Dower, slowly and carefully, so that I can take it in.'

She did as he had commanded, twice more, her eyes filled again, this time with tears of happiness.

'When?' he asked, lying on his side and stroking her stomach with reverent hands which had stormed the waistband of her skirt and invaded it.

'When did it happen? Oh, Leo, I can't think with you doing that!' His laugh was a gloating growl and he went on with his onslaught on her senses. 'That—that last night, I think.' She arched beneath his possessive hands. 'Please, Leo, wait, don't...' He paused for a fraction of a second. 'That last night I thought you'd taken precautions...'

'And I thought you had.'

'I'd forgotten. You'd shown so little interest in me that way that I'm afraid I lapsed.'

He pretended to be shocked at her oversight. 'Want the truth?' She nodded. 'I had to keep away from you, otherwise I'd have been making love to you every time I saw you. As it was, I could barely keep to my own room at night.'

'After—after that last time,' she massaged his shoulders beneath his unfastened shirt, 'where did you disappear to? It wasn't—tell me it wasn't to——?'

'My God, it wasn't to Sonya's. If you must know,' even now his eyes turned grim, 'I walked across the moors until I was exhausted, then slept in a barn at Timmy's place. He never knew. Nor did Jerome, who was sleeping there. Want to know why?' He held her to him as if she were made of priceless porcelain. 'I could hardly bear the thought of you gone from my life. My conscience told me I had to let you go, to lead your own life with the man of your choice...'

'But, darling,' she whispered huskily, 'the man of my choice had walked out on me, and to me it seemed as if the world had come to an end. Especially when it was confirmed about the baby.'

'My God, we've been fools! The baby. Wait till Timmy knows! He was shattered last time when he knew there wasn't going to be another Dower making an appearance on the scene.'

'I knew that, but he does know, Leo,' she answered happily, 'and he was delighted.'

'You told him before you told me?'

Rhea tried to straighten out the frown between his brows. 'I just had to tell someone. I thought you'd be annoyed and accuse me of trying to keep you. I thought—really thought it was Sonya you wanted.'

'Now I'll tell you the truth. Once Sonya was in my life. But even before I met you, she'd gone out of it. She helps Timmy and me with the office work. She came with me on my business jaunts to do likewise.'

'And in between, she's a designer?'

'She is. I make up some of her work in metal. Which is the only reason she's there sometimes. Talking of the forge, the moment I saw you——'

'No, no, that's my line,' she broke in mischievously. 'The moment I saw *you* I fell in love with you.'

'—standing in the doorway,' Leo continued, trailing his hand down her thighs, 'I knew you were the one for me. I'd found the only woman with whom I'd want to spend the rest of my life,' he added with a long and lingering kiss.

'You fell in love with *me*?' she asked, surfacing from it at last.

'I did. Oh, yes, I most certainly did. Which, to be totally honest with you, as you've been with me, is why I married you. OK?'

'OK,' she repeated, her eyes shining. 'But suppose I'd really been expecting Jerome's child?'

'If he hadn't wanted it, I'd have adopted it as my own. Now do you see how much I loved you?'

A long time later, as they sat on a low sofa in each other's arms, Leo asked, lips to her ear, 'Tell me, how does revenge taste now?'

'Very, very sweet,' she answered, lifting her face for his kiss. 'Not like revenge at all.'

'How about—like this?' he growled, carrying her back to the bed and making love to her all over again.

HARLEQUIN®

PRESENTS® *plus*

Meet Fin McKenzie, a woman used to dealing with all kinds of problems. Until she finds Jake Danvers asleep—and naked— in the wrong bed!

And then there's Leonie Priestley, pregnant and alone until Giles Kent, her dead fiancé's brother, tries to take control.

Fin and Leonie are just two of the passionate women you'll discover each month in Harlequin Presents Plus. And trust us, you won't want to miss meeting their men!

Watch for
PRIVATE LIVES by Carole Mortimer
Harlequin Presents Plus #1583
and
FORBIDDEN FRUIT by Charlotte Lamb
Harlequin Presents Plus #1584

Harlequin Presents Plus
The best has just gotten better!

Available in September wherever Harlequin books are sold.

Take 4 bestselling love stories FREE

Plus get a FREE surprise gift!

Calloway Corners

In September, Harlequin is proud to bring readers four involving, romantic stories about the Calloway sisters, set in Calloway Corners, Louisiana. Written by four of Harlequin's most popular and award-winning authors, you'll be enchanted by these sisters and the men they love!

MARIAH by Sandra Canfield
JO by Tracy Hughes
TESS by Katherine Burton
EDEN by Penny Richards

As an added bonus, you can enter a sweepstakes contest to win a trip to Calloway Corners, and meet all four authors. Watch for details in all Calloway Corners books in September.

Fifty red-blooded, white-hot, true-blue hunks from every
State in the Union!

Beginning in May, look for MEN MADE IN AMERICA!
Written by some of our most popular authors, these
stories feature fifty of the strongest, sexiest men, each
from a different state in the union!

Two titles available every other month at your favorite
retail outlet.

In September, look for:

DECEPTIONS by Annette Broadrick (California)
STORMWALKER by Dallas Schulze (Colorado)

In November, look for:

STRAIGHT FROM THE HEART by Barbara Delinsky
(Connecticut)
AUTHOR'S CHOICE by Elizabeth August (Delaware)

You won't be able to resist MEN MADE IN AMERICA!

HARLEQUIN ✦ PRESENTS®

A Year DOWN UNDER

In 1993, Harlequin Presents celebrates the land down under. In September, let us take you to Sydney, Australia, in AND THEN CAME MORNING by Daphne Clair, Harlequin Presents #1586.

Amber Wynyard's career is fulfilling—she doesn't need a man to share her life. Joel Matheson agrees... Amber doesn't need just *any* man—she needs him. But can the disturbingly unconventional Australian break down her barriers? Will Amber let Joel in on the secret she's so long concealed?

Share the adventure—and the romance—of A Year Down Under!

Available this month in
A Year Down Under

THE STONE PRINCESS
by Robyn Donald
Harlequin Presents #1577
Available wherever Harlequin books are sold.